T0118540

# NO GOD NO HELL NO CHURCHES NO SALOONS

*Kay Rose*

iUniverse, Inc.
Bloomington

No God, No Hell, No Churches, No Saloons



Certain characters in this work are historical figures, and certain events portrayed did take place. However, this is a work of fiction. All of the other characters, names, and events as well as all places, incidents, organizations, and dialogue in this novel are either the products of the author's imagination or are used fictitiously.If there are only a few historical figures or actual events in the novel, the disclaimer could name them.

iUniverse books may be ordered through booksellers or by contacting:

iUniverse
1663 Liberty Drive
Bloomington, IN 47403
www.iuniverse.com
1-800-Authors (1-800-288-4677)



ISBN: 978-1-4620-5918-8 (sc)
ISBN: 978-1-4620-5920-1 (hc)
ISBN: 978-1-4620-5919-5 (e)

Printed in the United States of America

iUniverse rev. date: 10/18/2011

# Introduction

Liberal, Missouri, was founded to be a "free thinking" town, with no God, no hell, no churches and no saloons. This colorful beginning, plus the spiritualist meetings that were held in Liberal, drew national attention. My grandma, Bertha Fast Palmer, lived in Liberal during this period of time. She witnessed the spiritualist meetings and the town being divided by the barb wire fence. Another town called Pedro was built just west of Liberal. Businesses and homes moved back and forth from Liberal to Pedro on a daily basis. These events are facts. I used grandma's family to create a personal story for more interest. It was not necessary to create much fiction when the facts were better. However, one fact remains; Christianity is alive and well in Liberal today. There are several churches and no saloons.

# Chapter 1

"No God, no hell, no churches, no saloons?" Mary Bouton slowly read the pamphlet her husband had handed to her. She took her eyes off of the pamphlet and stared at him with a puzzled look on her face. "Why would anyone want to live in a town with no churches or God?"

James brushed her question aside. "Oh, I'm sure that's just something in the advertisement. There's bound to be a lot of good people down there," he insisted.

Mary was quiet for a few minutes, studying her husband. James Bouton could be called a handsome man, tall, slender, with dark hair and dark eyes. Right at this moment, those dark eyes danced with excitement. This excitement suddenly made Mary nervous and fearful.

"Well, we have good people right here. Why would you even think of moving?"

"I'd just like to live in a town where it was just beginning. We'd sort of be like pioneers, with everything being new. Everyone would be working together, creating a brand new town." Pointing to the paper, he added, "It says that Liberal will be the perfect place to live. It's for progressive, intelligent people."

Shaking her head, Mary just walked away, leaving James to study the pamphlet.

Mary didn't share James's enthusiasm, but that was all he could talk about for several days. This piece of paper was starting to look worn since James was showing it to every person he met. The pamphlet had been written by a Mr. George Walser and sent all over the United States. It told of a new town, called Liberal, being built in southwest Missouri. This little pamphlet was certainly causing a lot of problems between Mary and her husband, Dr. James Bouton.

Their daughter, Bertha, heard them talking about Liberal almost every day. At least, she heard her pa talking about it. The only thing Bertha knew was that she didn't want to move and leave her family in Pleasant Hill. She was shy, and making new friends would be hard for her. She hoped her ma would say no to moving, but Ma didn't have much to say when the subject came up. Several days later, James was still talking about Liberal.

Finally, Mary shrugged her shoulders and agreed. "I guess you might as well go down there and see what this place looks like. I can tell that you have your mind set on going, and you can't seem to think of anything else ever since you saw that pamphlet."

How Bertha hated to hear her ma say it would be all right for her pa to go down to this new town. She didn't even want to think about moving there, but her pa was soon packing the wagon and getting ready to travel to Liberal to see what this area really looked like. James was very excited, but it was a sad day for everyone else. Mary and Bertha both cried when they said good-bye.

"Pa, why do you have to go? We need you to stay here with us," she told him while hugging his neck and hoping he'd change his mind and not leave.

Smiling and waving good-bye, he yelled, "Maybe they need a doctor down there in Liberal. I'll write soon and tell you everything I find out."

Bertha and Mary immediately started missing him as he drove the wagon down the lane, going off on his adventure to search out this new community. They both realized that perhaps changes were coming to their lives, and they were not happy about facing those changes.

Bertha was waving good-bye to her pa and holding her little brother Claude. *I wish I were little like Claude so I wouldn't even know what was going on in our family.*

Several weeks later, the letter that Mary, her parents, and Bertha were dreading to get came. Pa wrote that Liberal was a good place to call home, and he'd bought land there. A house was being built for them with a room for him to see his patients. It was on the southwest corner of College and Maple Street, just a block from Main Street. "Businesses are moving in every day, and it will be very convenient for you and the children to walk to town and get your staples," he wrote. Next, he described Mr. George Walser, the founder of Liberal, as a very intelligent, wealthy man whom he liked very much, although he did have some controversial ideas.

Mary and Bertha sure didn't share James's excitement about moving, and neither did Mary's parents. After reading the letter out loud, Mary just sat there in the chair, with tears dropping all over the paper as they streamed down her face.

"Ma, are we really going to move? Can't you tell Pa that we don't want to?" Bertha's lip quivered. "You know I get scared when I meet new people. I want to stay here."

Mary had a lot of important things to visit with her parents about, so she told Bertha's older cousin to take her outside to play. As Bertha walked out the back door, she saw Ma and her grandparents, just sitting on the sofa, looking sad. *I know they are going to talk about us moving, and they don't want me to be sad too.*

---

The Bouton family moved to Liberal, and the years passed quickly. Good things and bad things had happened since moving. Bertha was out in the yard, hanging up the washing and daydreaming as she often did. *I lost one brother but got two new ones.* All of a sudden, Bertha knew it was time to quit daydreaming about the past and think about today and her chores. Wearily, picking up the last clean towel that Ma had just washed, she hung it over the clothesline. Turning her attention from the clothes basket, she looked off behind the house, where the prairie grass was waving in the wind. It was as high as Pa's shoulders. Each house had a small yard and was surrounded by the tall grass. Deep, rutted paths were what the residents called streets, but they didn't seem like streets to her. However, they all did lead to Main Street, where businesses were being built almost every day as people came moving in from just about everywhere. The warm Missouri breezes were whipping the clothes dry, so it would soon be her job to take the clothes back to the house. With no other girls in the family, Bertha kept busy, helping her ma with all of the chores. Tomorrow would be mending day, and Ma was teaching her how to sew new shirts for Wally and Harry.

Her brother Wally had been told to watch little brother Harry, while she and Ma did the washing. Glancing around the yard, she saw them playing by the tall grass.

"Wally," she yelled, "you make sure you watch Harry and don't let him wander off in the prairie. He could get lost out there, and we'd have a time finding him."

When she yelled at Wally to watch Harry, her words suddenly triggered memories of that terrible wash day when little Claude had died. Instantly, tears sprang up and started to run down her cheeks, with big sobs jerking out of her chest. If only she'd been watching Claude a little closer, he'd probably be right there, grinning at her as he handed her clothes to hang on the line. She looked up to heaven and silently prayed, *God, if you are up there, please help me 'cause wash days are so hard.* The horrible memories always keep pushing up in her mind.

Pa seemed to keep busy with his patients and hardly mentioned little Claude anymore, but she and Ma always had lots of trouble facing wash days. Just standing there crying, she didn't hear Ma come up behind her till she felt her loving arms around her. Startled, she turned and saw that Ma was crying too.

Seemed like wash days always brought heaviness to them. It's like big black clouds were hovering over their heads. They just stood in the yard, hugging each other, not saying anything for a while. Then they just looked at each other, knowing what was going through their minds.

"Now hush, it wasn't your fault. It just happened, and you've got to quit your fretting," Ma whispered. "Now finish these clothes and come on in. I've got warm bread and jam for you to eat." Patting her back, she added, "Eating will be good for you. You've lost so much flesh that you don't even make a good shadow."

Wiping her eyes with her apron, Bertha replied, "But, Ma, I just miss Claude so much."

"I know, honey, so do I, but we got to go on living, you know. Little Claude's all right. He's with Jesus. It's you I'm worried about."

She nodded. "I'll go fetch the boys, and we'll be in to eat bread and jam in a minute."

Slowly, Mary Bouton walked back to the house, with her shoulders drooping and her feet feeling as heavy as lead. Trying to cheer up her daughter was hard. Claude's death was a terrible burden for a young girl to bear, and it seemed like Bertha just couldn't find much happiness anymore. *But how can I cheer her up, when I have so much pain and guilt myself?*

As her ma went back in the house, Bertha again looked up to the sky, wondering if Claude was watching down from heaven, smiling at her. *Dear Jesus, if you can hear me, tell Claude I'm so sorry. Tell him that I love him and I sure do miss him a whole lot.*

Tugging on her dress, Wally was standing right beside her, looking up with questioning eyes.

"What's the matter, Bertha? Are you hurting bad?"

"Never mind, Wally, just bring Harry in 'cause Ma's got hot bread right out of the oven and homemade jam for us to eat. Then we'll get your reader out and I'll listen to you recite."

As Bertha came in the house, she heard Pa and Ma talking in low tones. That usually meant they were saying things that the children didn't need to hear. Feeling a little guilty at eavesdropping on her parents' conversation, she stepped back but then stood quietly and listened.

"James, I'm really worried about Bertha. I wish you'd take a look at the girl. She's looking poorly. Do you suppose she has the consumption or something?"

"Well, swan to mercy; you've probably just been working her too hard. All you and the children been doing is spring-cleaning. Seems like it's been going on for days."

"Well, you don't want a dirty house, do you? Would you have any patients coming in if the place was filthy?"

"No, but you've been washing and scrubbing and dragging out the carpets and then dragging them back in for days and days."

Mary laughed. "You saw how much fun Wally was having, hitting the dirt out of the rugs with that old rug beater, didn't you? He didn't even know he was working. And he didn't know it was work when I had him put coal oil on those feathers and rub it around the edge of the floor."

"I know, I know," James agreed, "and I have to admit that your feather and coal oil idea is keeping the bugs out, even if it did stink up the house. Working is not hurting Wally. He thinks he's the biggest toad in the puddle, but I know its Bertha you're stewing about." After pausing for a moment, he continued, "I've been studying on it and have an idea. Why don't you take the children on the train and go up and visit your family for a few weeks? It'd do you and Bertha both some good to get away from here for a while."

The thought of seeing her family put a big smile on Mary's face. "Yes, I'd love to see Mama and Papa and Sister Helen and all of her kids, but can't you come with us? That's a long ride on that train, trying to keep those two boys sitting still and behaving."

"I just can't up and leave these sick folks all alone, now can I? You know Mr. Jones's leg is still full of poisoning and Mrs. Guffy is having those bad spells all the time. Bertha can help with the boys and I'll go another time."

"I think I'm putting too much work on Bertha, like she's the boys' mama, instead of their sister. She's not having any fun anymore, like young folks should be having, at least once in a while. Seems like she just can't get over Claude's death, even after all of these years."

"Well, send her up to the store for an errand and tell her to stop and visit some friends before coming home. I saw that coffee was ten cents a pound. Tell her to buy us some."

Just then they saw Bertha and quickly quit their talking. "Come in, Bertha," her pa said, motioning for her to sit down. "Just look what your ma has fixed for us to eat." Walking over to her, he gave her a quick hug and had her pull up a chair beside him. Moments later, the brothers came bursting into the room, looking for the food they were promised.

"Is this the jam you made from those blackberries we picked down by the railroad track?" Wally asks, grabbing for bread with his dirty little hands.

"Sure is. If you and Bertha hadn't gone down there and picked those berries, we'd be eating plain old bread today, without any jam. I've got fresh churned butter too," his ma announced. "Now you take Harry and go back out to the pump and wash that dirt off your hands before you eat."

As they sat down at the kitchen table, Wally beamed, knowing that he helped with the jam, and quickly started shoving bread into his mouth. Dr. Bouton smiled, enjoying watching his boys gobbling down their food. Bertha just sat quietly, eating her snack and thinking about what she'd heard Pa and Ma talking about. *Sounds like we might be taking a trip to see Grandpa and Grandma. Maybe that would be good. It would be nice to see all the family up at Pleasant Hill. If I'm gone, I wouldn't have to hear about all the folks in Liberal fussing with each other. The freethinkers don't like the Christians moving in their town. And the Christians call the freethinkers infidels and atheists and are shouting that they are all going to hell. Ma has remarked several times that this town was just as stirred up as a hornet's nest.* Bertha slowly buttered more bread, still daydreaming. She noticed that Pa didn't say much about either side. *Seems like he sort of wants to just stay out of all the fussing and feuding that is going on.* Thinking back to that awful day, when Claude was dying, she remembered Pa going out in the backyard, falling on his knees, and crying out to God. In between sobs, she remembered Pa pleading with God. His very words were, "Don't punish this little boy for my sins." He must be a believer or he wouldn't have been praying, but he sure keeps his beliefs to himself. How she'd like to ask Pa what terrible sin he was talking about, but she didn't dare. He didn't seem like a sinner to her. You couldn't ask for a better Pa, even if he wasn't her real pa. Ma was a believer and every time she'd get the Bible out to read to her and Wally, Pa would usually remember something he needed to tend to outside. It didn't seem like Pa was a freethinker either, but he sure must like ole Mr. Walser since he insisted that they name Wally after him. He said it was the only fitting thing to do since Wally was the first boy born in the town of Liberal, so he was named George Walser Bouton. Too bad that her other brother, little Claude, became the first person to be buried in Liberal. How she wished it was her buried instead of Claude. Bertha felt like her life had almost stopped that day, but she was still alive, always having to remember those terrible memories.

"Bertha, I do believe your hearing is bad. I've been talking to you, and you're just staring out in space like you didn't even hear a word I said. I'm needing you to go down to Brown's Dry Good Store and pick out some lace for that new dress I'm sewing for you." Mary motioned for Bertha to go into the bedroom. "Go change to your street dress, and I'll get a scrap of material for you to match up with the lace."

"Get me a pound of coffee too. Mr. Brown has it on sale this week" Pa called to her.

"Ma, let me go," Wally chimed in. "I can skedaddle down there quick, and I could run past the watering trough and see who is coming past to water their teams.

"No, Wally, I want Bertha to pick out the colors. Boys don't know much about lace and colors. You stay here and let your pa hear you read for him this afternoon. If you read well, later I'll let you go down to the well and visit with the travelers that are stopping to get water."

"Last week I talked to three families that were going clear to Kansas. That's a far piece, isn't it, Ma? I saw a covered wagon that had 'Kansas or bust' written on it and they sure had a bunch of stuff in their wagon."

"Probably had everything they owned in that wagon. When your pa and I came to Liberal, we sure had our wagon full too."

Bertha just sat there, not really wanting to go to town. Wally sure liked to go to town, but she didn't share his enthusiasm. She knew Ma and Pa were just trying to cheer her up and were thinking up excuses to get her out of the house and to go see people. It was hard to go anywhere. She always felt like folks were staring at her when she went down to the stores.Guess they were just feeling sorry for her and whispering about little Claude dying. But she did want some lace for her dress, so she slowly got up and headed to the bedroom to change her clothes. Brushing her long brown hair, she rolled it up in a bun. *I better buy some Borax too. We used all we had last month when we washed our hair, and it's almost time to do it again.*

"You don't need to hurry home," Ma called. "Stop by and visit some of your friends, and show them what your new dress will be looking like soon as I get it done. Harry and I are going to rest a spell and Pa can help Wally with his reader."

Slowly, Bertha walked to town, trying to miss stepping in all of the mud puddles and horse piles. *Someday*, she thought, *I'm going to move away from here and live in a big city, where the streets are bricks and my shoes won't get covered with mud every time I walk to town.* After buying the lace, she remembered that Ma suggested for her to stop and visit a friend before coming home. She quickly knew the friend she wanted to visit would be Rosa Fast. Going past Rosa's house after shopping seemed to be a good idea. Smiling a little, she wondered if Rosa's brother, William, might be home. It seemed like William always found reasons to come in the house when she was visiting Rosa. In the Fast parlor, there was a special corner, where Rosa and Bertha usually sat, embroidering on their tea towels they were making for Christmas gifts. Sometimes they did more talking and giggling than embroidering. However, Bertha always kept her eye out for William. He'd walk past two or three times before Rosa would call for him to come over and see what they were doing. Although William was a few years older than Bertha, he was rather bashful, so he'd stand around, looking at their tea towels, trying to think up something to say. He was pleasant to look at, with a friendly smile, and his brown hair was usually poking out from under his work hat. He was a very kind person, always working hard, helping others, and everyone spoke highly of him. Rosa always teased her about coming to see William instead of her. *Well, maybe she's right, but I'm not admitting it. Well, at least not today. There are several things I don't like about Liberal, but William and Rosa are two good reasons for living here. Being with them makes me happy.* Walking quickly, she was anxious to get to the Fast home and see her friends.

# Chapter 2

"James would you and Wally run out to the chicken pen and pick out a good fryer for the noon meal, 'cause I've invited company to come sit and eat with us," Mary announced at the breakfast table.

"Whose coming past, Ma?" Wally inquired as he smacked up the last bite of Johnny cake. "I ran in to Kate Hesford up at Mohlers Mercantile the other day. She scolded me good about us not getting together to visit anymore. Said she hadn't seen me in a coon's age, so I told her when she comes back to town to do her trading, we'd fix fried chicken for her."

"Oh boy! Can we have mashed taters and lots of good ole gravy and sweet corn and some of our new jam for the bread?"

"Yes and maybe we'll have custard if you will check and see if that old hen has started laying again, but first, bring in some coal for the oven and help your pa catch that fryer."

Grabbing the ax and starting out to the chicken pen, James was sure glad to see Mary start to visit with her lady friends again. Silently he wished that Bertha would start wanting to visit with her friends again too. That would be a good sign they might be starting to heal up from their grief. *Maybe they'll start going to the quilting bee again, now that company's coming.*

Mary yelled at her son as he went out the back door. "Wally, keep out of that chicken's way till its done flopping around. Last time you got blood all over your trousers, and I can't get the stains out."

"Stains don't hurt nothing, Ma. These here are my old trousers anyway."

"Well, you can turn your good trousers into your old ones in about five seconds, so try to keep these looking good till after company leaves." Turning to Bertha, she says, "It's the beatenist thing how that boy can get his clothes so dirty."

Bertha was still eating her breakfast, not saying much as usual. Turning to her daughter Mary says, "Kate is bringing Alice in with her today. Said she wanted you to help her with some embroidering. She's not much interested in doing it and thought maybe you could help by getting her started with a tea towel. You can start one for your hope chest too."

Nodding yes, she realized that Ma was trying to get her back into seeing folks again, but that's all right, she thought. "We need a few more strands of colors. I saw them on sale at Browns Dry Goods for a penny each. Should I go down there and buy three or four more colors?"

"Yes, ask your pa to give you a dime and you can buy me some white thread too. Kate wants to show me a new quilt top she's working on, and maybe I'll start us one just like it. You know we've got lots of scraps of material we need to use up. While Alice is here, I'll get you girls to cut pieces for me. Maybe you girls can start your very own quilts. You can't have too many quilts for your hope chest." Mary quit chattering when she saw Bertha showing some interest in having company come to the house.

As Bertha started to town, Wally came chasing after her. "Wait for me. Ma said I could go along and pick out a penny piece of candy. That's my pay for watching Harry today while you women sew."

---

Patting Mary on the shoulder, James smiled at her and declared, "That's the best fried chicken I've ever tasted in all my born days, Mrs. Bouton. Now if you folks will excuse me, I'll leave the dishes to you and be about my business, but I sure want to invite you ladies back again real soon." James walked out the door to hitch up the team to the buck board, smiling. *It's good seeing Mary and Bertha enjoying time with their friends. Now if I can just get them to go visit up at Pleasant Hill, I can put my plans into action.*

Kate insisted that they help clean up the kitchen before they started sewing. As Bertha started to throw away the chicken bones, Alice yelled at her, "Don't throw that wish bone away. Put it over your door!"

Bertha was puzzled. "Why in the world would I put an old wishbone over my door? Have you taken leave of your mind?"

"No, not at all. The kids at Coal Valley School say if you put a wishbone over the door, the first boy who comes through the door will be the one you'll marry," Alice replied.

"Well, I can tell you who will be busting through that doorway about a hundred times a day. It's Wally, and he is usually having a conniption over something he just seen around town."

Alice pointed out the rules. "Your kin doesn't count. It's got to be some fellar that's not your brother or uncle or pa."

Still amused at her young friend, she cleaned off the wishbone at Alice's insistence. "All right, I'll do it for you, but I don't believe it'll work." They all walked into the parlor and watched Bertha nail it over the front door.

Shaking her head, Mary laughed. "It'll probably be ole Pinky Jones or Mr. Walser who comes through the door."

Alice seriously explained, "It's got to be someone not married. Old married fellows or your kin don't count."

The wishbone was soon forgotten, and the girls went to the parlor to start on their tea towels. The older ladies were walking back to the kitchen when Mary happened to look out the back window and saw James out by the wagon, talking to two men.

"If that don't beat all. James Roberts and W. S. Van Camp are here again," she muttered to Kate in a low voice. "They've been stopping past almost every day. All three of them, have their heads together whispering. When I ask him what they want, he shrugs his shoulders and says, 'It's just business.'"

Coming over to take a look out the window, Kate commented, "What business would those two scalawags have with the doctor unless they were sick? And they sure don't look poorly to me."

"No, they look fit as a fiddle, but something is going on that's making me all fired wondering about these meetings."

As they stood peering out the window, Kate broke the silence. "Don't suppose they want to borrow money from James, do you?"

"Can't be that. We never seem to have much extra money. James has wanted to send me and the youngins up to see my family, so it'll take all the dollars we have for the train fares."

Kate teased, "Maybe he is going to take up fife lessons from ole W. S. You know how he sits in front of his old shack down on Main Street, blowing that fife in the evening, probably dreaming about the times he played during the Civil War. I saw a mouth harp on sale at McIntosh's Hardware for ten cents, so guess you'll have to buy one for James."

The men finished their conversation. Roberts and Van Camp walked away as James drove off in his buckboard.

"I can't figure out what's going on, but it sure makes a body wonder."

Returning to the parlor to sew, Kate asks, "What do you think about this new town being built right beside Liberal?"

"I hear the Christians are all moving over there and calling it Dennison. One day someone lives in Liberal, and the next day, they have a conniption fit and move over to Dennison," Mary pointed out.

"What side is James on?"

Thinking a little while, Mary paused. "I don't really seem to know his thoughts on freethinking and Walser's ideas. He likes to keep his ideas private, but all of this town's feuding is upsetting me a whole lot. Wish things would just settle down."

"I guess you've heard about this new preacher, Braden Clark, coming to town to preach to the infidels, haven't you? He says that someone wrote for him to come to Liberal and save the town," Kate continued.

"Yes, Mr. Harmon knew him back in Illinois and said Clark was an infidel himself. Supposedly had an experience with Jesus, just like the Apostle Paul, and now he says he's called to preach to the Liberal residents. Calls the people immoral and grossly wicked. He's put out a pamphlet that says those very words."

"Bet that makes a lot of folks fiery mad to be called immoral and grossly wicked," Kate commented. "Especially Mr. Walser. Now Preacher Clark and Mr. Stewart are having these debates over Christianity and freethinking, and that's got lots of the people thinking about how they're living."

"Bully for them. It's about time someone around here started thinking about their actions."

"Do you suppose Walser wished he'd never started this town and just stayed in Lamar, being a smart lawyer?" Kate wondered.

"I doubt it. You remember he bought all of this land real cheap 'cause someone had plotted it as swamp land. I'm guessing he is certainly enjoying his bargain."

"Wasn't that quite a trick to get this prairie declared swamp land?" Kate remarked.

"Imagine leading citizens signing an affidavit, saying that they'd ridden over this part of the country in a boat."

Both women laughed at the same time. "They just forgot to mention that the boat was fastened up on a wagon. Guess it just sailed right over the prairie grass with no problems, except a team of mules happened to be pulling the wagon."

Pointing to the newspaper on the table, Mary spoke sharply, "That paper right there keeps things stirred up. I don't even like to read it anymore."

"Since Walser owns the paper, he can write whatever he wants in it. I hear Liberal is receiving attention from all over the United States, and Walser is probably enjoying every minute of it. Another thing I heard is just last week he and seven men formed the Spiritual Science Association, whatever that means," Kate remarked. "They must be his strongest followers."

"I heard about that group's organization, and I was surely glad that James didn't join them," Mary sighed. "At least I don't think he joined, but I'm not sure."

"Wonder why Walser is on such a crusade against Christians?"

"I hear that Walser was raised in a church that taught John Calvin's doctrines, but something sure caused him to change his mind, and it's made him bitter about Christianity," Mary declared.

"He must still have some Christian thoughts," Kate suggested. "Just look how he laid out the cemetery with him wanting to be buried in the center circle."

Mary bristled. "Oh yes, he wants all the rest of us to be buried around that circle, with our feet toward him so that when we are resurrected, we'll all rise up facing him, saying he's a great leader."

"Doesn't sound like infidel thinking to me if he's planning on being resurrected. Sounds like he's remembering some of his Bible teachings."

Just then Wally came in from the front yard and was so excited he could hardly talk. "Come quick, there's a house going right down the street."

All the ladies jumped up, leaving their sewing projects, and ran to the windows. Sure enough, there went a team of mules past, pulling a house on skids.

"Look at the sign on the back. It says, 'and the Lord Said: Get thee Out of Sodom.'"

Kate sighed. "Well, there goes one more family moving from Liberal to Dennison. Guess they're tired of listening to all this name-calling. Hmm, maybe Liberal is Sodom."

"Someday, Walser may be sitting here in Liberal, in his perfect town, all by himself," Mary snapped as they sat back down and continued their sewing.

In just a few more minutes, Wally came busting through the doorway again, yelling, "Bertha, guess who's stopping his wagon out front and saying he'd like to speak to you? It's William Fast. Wonder what he wants to see you about?"

The girls leaped up from their sewing and quickly looked out the front window. "Hush, Wally, he'll hear you," Bertha snapped at her brother. Looking at Alice, she whispered, "Land a mercy, what's he doing here?"

Prodding her daughter, Mary said, "Well, Bertha, go to the door and invite him in. Don't leave him standing out on the steps."

Just as Bertha went to open the door, they all looked up at the wishbone and burst into laughter. Poor William didn't know what to think when he was greeted by a room full of giggling women. Bertha's face turned as red as the red flower she was embroidering on the tea towel, and she couldn't get a word to come out of her mouth.

Finally, Mary spoke up. "Nice to see you, William. Do come in."

Fumbling for words, William said, "Well, my sister Rosa knew I'd be passing your way, and she wanted me to stop and ask Bertha if she would like to go to the preaching with us tonight." Looking her way, he said, "Said to tell you she sure wanted you to join her if you could."

At that moment, Bertha wished that the floor would just open up and let her fall through. Just seeing William in her parlor was almost more than she could stand, but watching Alice grinning from ear to ear and looking up at that wishbone was just too much. William stood there, shuffling his feet and looking puzzled at Kate and Bertha.

Mary finally broke the silence. "Why, that's right nice of Rosa to be thinking of Bertha." Then glancing at Bertha, she said, "That's a good way for you to spend tonight, don't you think?"

All Bertha could do was nod her head yes, and it was settled that she'd be going to church with Rosa and her family that night.

William moved back and forth, looking at the floor. "Fine, we'll be stopping at about six thirty for you. I'd best be going on now. See you tonight."

As he walked out into the yard, Mary called, "Tell Rosa thanks for inviting Bertha." Then she turned around, and they all looked up at the wishbone and burst into laughter again.

"Be still, he'll hear you," Bertha scolded.

---

The Hesfords left later that afternoon, and Bertha was busy putting on her new dress for the services. After James came home, it was plain to hear that her pa wasn't very happy about Mary giving her permission to attend the preaching.

"Well, you were the one who said she needs to get out and be with her friends again," Mary said firmly. "The Fasts are good people, and it'll be nice for her to go somewhere instead of sitting around the house with us every night."

"Dag blame it, I hear that new preacher is shouting hell, fire, and brimstone, and Bertha don't need to be hearing all that stuff."

"I'd rather her hear some good preaching than all of that nonsense that Walser is trying to cram into our minds," Mary snapped at him. "Besides, it made Bertha real happy to have William stop past, and I've already told her she could go. If you don't want her to go, you'll have to tell her yourself."

"All right," he conceded, "but one of these nights we'll be taking our family to one of Walser's debates. And then she can decide a few things for herself."

The discussion ended as Wally came into the parlor, dancing around, calling for everyone to come see Bertha. "She's got on her new blue dress that Ma made her, and she sure looks pretty. Look how she's dun combed her hair, taking it out of that big ole knot on her head."

Bertha was blushing and really wanting Wally to be still. She never liked to be the center of attention. It had been quite a while since Bertha had looked so happy, so James sat down and decided to quit fussing about her going to the church services. He did love that girl and her happiness was important to him. Looking at her, he remembered the day she found out that he wasn't her real pa. They were packing to move to Liberal, and their neighbor came over to help. In a whisper so loud that Bertha could hear her, the old lady asked Mary if Bertha knew her real pa was dead. He could still see little Bertha jumping up and running across the room, grabbing him by the leg and crying. "My pa ain't dead. He's right here beside me." He regretted that day that his stepdaughter found out he wasn't her real pa, especially hearing it from that old biddy. Just thinking about her sticking her nose in his family's life still made him angry. *Why didn't she tend to her own business and keep her nose out of my family's business?* The old biddy quickly vamoosed, but the damage was done. He never intended for Bertha to know that she wasn't her real pa. But now, years later, that conversation was never mentioned by any of the family.

It seems that she's just as much his daughter, as if she was his own flesh and blood. That's just the way James wanted it to be too. When he married Mary, he took that girl, too, just as his very own. *Guess I might as well let her go 'cause she's almost grown, but I just don't like the idea of her hearing a lot of nonsense from that preacher.*

# Chapter 3

KEEPING ONE EYE ON the front door and the other eye on the clock, it was a tense evening for James and Mary. Waiting for Bertha to come home from the preaching was all they could think about. James pretended to be interested in reading the newspaper, making comments to Mary.

"Listen to this? *The Lamar Democrat* says that a Mr. and Mrs. Alott bought a folding bed and they proceeded to occupy it. The bed folded up with them inside, and Mr. Alott was seriously injured, and Mrs. Alott was most dangerously injured."

"Land sakes!" Mary exclaimed. "That is what I wanted to buy for the boys."

For the first time that evening, James laughed. "I can just see our boys all tangled up in that bed like a sandwich."

"Don't make fun of it. What if we'd bought one of those beds and our boys got hurt? I'm sure glad we didn't buy one."

"Well, it says these people are suing the bed makers."

"Hope the judge gives the dear lady some money and she gets well."

It was obvious that James was trying to make small talk and act like he wasn't upset about Bertha going with the Fasts to preaching, but Mary could tell otherwise. His face was tense; he kept tapping his shoe on the floor and drumming his fingers on the table. Picking up the paper several times, he pretended to be interested in the news. Mary also felt nervous and was trying to think of something to talk about.

"Wally sure likes to go down to the water pump and visit with folks," she remarked. "The other day he talked with people who have gone out west and now have come back. Said that moving west wasn't so wonderful after all."

The clock on the mantel ticked away with Mary and James sitting quietly. It was fine with her for Bertha to hear what the preacher had to say, but Mary didn't want to see James upset. *I couldn't ask for a better husband and father for the children.* She was just getting ready to tell James how she felt, when the door opened.

Bertha walked in, kept her head down, and murmured, "Good night," and quickly headed to the bedroom she shared with her brothers. Red, puffy eyes were a sure sign that she'd been crying.

James and Mary just stared at each other, neither one speaking a word. James stood up and gave Mary an I-told-you-so look and stomped off to bed.

Tears filled Mary's eyes. *Have I made a big mistake in letting Bertha go to the preaching?*

---

The rooster was crowing in the backyard, announcing daybreak, but Mary beat him up this morning. James never said one word to her all night long, and she could feel his stiff body being careful not to touch hers. Not knowing how the breakfast conversation might go, she decided to let the boys sleep awhile. Bertha came to the kitchen to help cook as usual and said nothing. James joined them at the table, glancing at Mary, waiting for their daughter to comment about the preaching.

Slowly eating and not looking up, Bertha finally broke the silence.

"Did you know the Bible says Jesus will give you peace that passes all understanding?"

Again, James and Mary looked at each other, a little shocked at how she had started the conversation.

"Yes, that's in the Bible," Mary replied, "but so many folks, including me, don't seem to apply that Scripture to their lives."

"Well, Rosa knew that I've been hurting on my insides for a long time, fretting about Claude and how I should have been watching him better, so she had Preacher Clark pray for me to have peace."

Interrupting, James reached over for her hand. "We've had this conversation a hundred times, and we've told you it wasn't your fault. You were busy sorting clothes and didn't know your ma had stepped out to the well to get a bucket of cold water, when Claude went tumbling into that tub of boiling water."

"I was right there in the room with him, and I've had a terrible time trying to forget his screaming and how I pulled his poor little scalded body out of that water." Mary and James sat quietly, waiting for her to continue speaking. Pausing a little while, she stated, "I believe that last night will be the last time I cry about Claude. When they prayed for me, I felt a big heavy load lift off of my back. I've got Jesus with me now, and I've got his peace. I'm going to forgive myself, and when I think of Claude, I'll only remember the cute little things he said and did. I'm thanking Jesus for taking him to heaven, and someday, I'll see him and get to give him a great big hug." Smiling, she looked at her parents.

Tears were running down James's and Mary's face as they looked at each other. This was one time when James could not say a word. Bertha was finally getting peace about Claude's death, and that was just exactly what he wanted for her.

Pleading, Bertha asked, "Can we all go back to the preaching tonight?" Looking at her ma, she added, "You've been hurting a long time too. Go with me tonight and get some peace, like Preacher Clark talks about."

Just then Wally came bouncing into the kitchen, claiming he was starving. James quickly remembered something he needed to do, mumbling about feeding the mules, so the conversation was over for a while.

Bertha waited all day for her ma to discuss whether she would go to the preaching that night. Earlier, Bertha saw her parents having a visit out in the backyard. She was hoping they would come in and announce that they'd all be going together. However, James came in and announced that he was driving out to the DeLissa Ranch, because Mr. DeLissa sent word his wife was suffering from an attack of the grip. Wally immediately wanted to accompany his pa since he'd heard talk of Mr. DeLissa having a new team of oxen.

Jumping up and down with excitement, he clamored, "I heard those oxen came from clear up by Fort Scott, and they are mighty big critters. Let me go get a good look at them, Pa. I'll be the only boy who has got to go see them."

Mary came into the room and overheard the conversation about a little trip outside of town.

"If that boy goes, you make sure you keep your eyes on him. You know how he is in one spot now, and a minute later, he's somewhere else."

Looking at oxen was the last thing Mary wanted to hear about. James looked at her face and saw the pain she was feeling, just hearing the word oxen mentioned. She had seen her first husband trampled by one, and the thought of Wally being excited over them was not pleasing her at all.

"I'll watch him. Let him go and have a good time."

Mary nodded all right, but James could see her standing in the doorway, watching them go, tugging on her apron like she always did when she was fretting.

Bertha was glad to see them drive away. Now, hopefully, she thought her ma would talk about tonight. They sat in the parlor, working on the new quilt for a few minutes, when Mary broke the silence.

"Your pa says he won't stand in our way of going to the preaching tonight, but he wants us to go up to the Mental Liberty Hall with him one night and hear those debates."

Rolling her eyes, Bertha answered, "But, Ma, some of the kids say those debates are just a bunch of fancy words about absolutely nothing."

"Well, I guess we can listen for ourselves and decide if it's anything we might find of interest. I hear they have scientists, philosophers, and those seven teachers from The Liberal Free Thought University speak real often."

"I don't really think Pa is a freethinker. Do you?"

"No, I don't think so either," she says, shaking her head, "but he doesn't want to talk about his beliefs or his past, as you well know."

"Why is that, Ma?"

"I don't really know, but we both know he is a good man, so I don't try to pry into something he doesn't want to talk about."

Later, Bertha glanced out the window and saw Pa and Wally driving in the yard.

"Look at the way Wally is running to the house. Looks like a cyclone is after him."

"You know that boy never has walked anywhere, always running every step he takes. He must be excited from seeing the oxen."

Racing into the front room, yelling, "Ma, Bertha, guess what we just saw on the way home?" Not giving anyone a chance to reply, he said, "Ole Mr. Walser and a bunch of his buddies are building a tall fence to keep the Christians out of Liberal."

"Now Wally, are you sure you saw a fence being built?" Mary asked.

"Yes, Pa and I stopped to watch them build it, and I heard Mr.

Walser laugh and tell Pa that it would keep the Christians out of Liberal. Said it was too low for them to crawl under and too high to crawl over and too many barbs to crawl through it. Said the Christians would just sit down and cry. Said the fence would save Liberal." Wally was completely out of breath after that big story, so he sat down to rest awhile. Bertha looked at her ma, shaking her head. "Do you think this fussing will ever stop?"

After quite a while, James finally came in the house, trying to look busy and fiddling with his doctoring bag.

"Well, Wally certainly had a lot of news to tell us," Mary pointed out. "Is it true that Walser is building a fence to keep Christians out of Liberal?"

"Yes, I guess he is, but don't fret about it. It won't be bothering us at all. We can still do our trading just like we always do, and it probably will come down soon anyway."

Quickly changing the subject, James commented, "Wally sure enjoyed our little trip today. He watched them working with the oxen and listened to DeLissa talk about being offered a bid on their land. This is causing quite a bit of excitement among the ranchers. Everyone I've talked to sure thinks land is really going to get high priced around here."

"DeLissa has been offered $51.25 an acre for some of his land and $65 an acre if he'd sell all of his 1,400 acres."

"Who'd pay that kind of price?" Mary wondered. "And to think it's supposed to be swamp land."

"Some fellow from New York is doing the bidding, but we're all guessing he's working for the railroad."

"Speaking of the railroad, I heard down at Brown's Dry Goods that some railroad men are coming to Dennison, calling a meeting, and trying to get them to change the town's name to something else. Said they had one stop at Dennison, Texas, and it was causing confusion to have another stop with the same name, even if it was a long way off in Missouri."

James had also heard about the meeting. "I might go over and just listen to what is being said. Since the depot is called Pedro, I'm guessing they will want to rename the town Pedro."

"It's foolish to have North Dennison and South Dennison right next door to Liberal.

If folks would get along and quit this fussing, we could have one nice peaceful community," Mary declared.

All of the problems in Liberal were something James tried to avoid talking about with his family, so he was glad to see Bertha come out of the bedroom, ending the conversation.

She was already dressed to go to the preaching. He knew she was happy about going, but it was plain to see that she was uncomfortable, knowing how he felt about the preaching. But he had said he wouldn't stop them from getting in with the Fasts and riding to the preaching meeting.

---

It was quite late when Bertha and Mary got home from the church services. They'd been hoping that James would have stayed up to hear about the evening. It was a wonderful service, full of prayer and worshiping. Sharing it with him was what they really planned to do. Since he was already to bed, it appeared that he was not interested in hearing anything they had to say.

"I sure wish we could talk to Pa right now."

"I do too, but we best not wake him up. I'll visit with him in the morning. You go get a good night's rest." Hugging her daughter, and smiling, she added, "We can sleep good tonight with Jesus's peace, can't we?

# Chapter 4

Loud words woke Bertha up from a good night's sleep. She could not believe this was her pa shouting. Listening, she quickly realized he was very upset about her and Ma enjoying the preaching last night.

"I don't want you and Bertha going to any more preaching. They've just put foolishness in your minds," he yelled.

Mary responded hotly, "How can you say such a thing? You've wanted us to get over Claude's death, and now that we've found a way to start healing, you want us to stop."

Slipping to the door, Bertha's chest got tight, hearing her parents quarrel. This was something that they just never did. *What's the matter with Pa? It's like someone else is in his body.*

James saw her and motioned for her to come in the room. Pointing his finger at her, his hand was shaking with anger. "I've just told your Ma and now I'm telling you that I don't want you to be around Rosa and William anymore. I'm going to enroll you in the Free Thought University and let you meet other young folks. There are plenty of other young folks around here besides them."

"But, Pa, Rosa and I have been friends for a long time. How can I stop being her friend?"

Spitting the words out, he replied, "You heard what I said. We're through talking about this subject. No preaching and no Rosa and William." He walked out the door, slamming it so hard the whole room shook, leaving Mary and Bertha standing in the middle of the room, staring at each other.

"What in the world has happened to Pa?"

By then, tears were streaming down Mary's face. "That's a good question. I've never seen him this way before."

"Rosa is my friend, and I really like William. How can I tell them I can't see them anymore?"

Trying to be strong, she grabbed her daughter's hand. "This is the time when we need to start praying for your pa. Remember last night they said that nothing is impossible with God? That's what we are going to start believing right now."

After praying, Bertha ran back to bed, pulled the sheet over her head, and sobbed for a long time. *God, I thought things were getting better, and now everything is worse.* She remembered last night, when William had whispered to her, asking if it'd be all right for him to come over and ask Pa if he could start seeing her. *He sure can't ask Pa anything today.*

The morning seemed long, with Mary and Bertha talking very little. Their minds and hearts were a long way from the kitchen, but they went through the motions of fixing their dinner. Wally came in with a message from Pa, saying he had places to go, so he wouldn't be taking the noon meal today. No words were spoken, but Mary and Bertha looked at each other, relieved that they wouldn't have to see Pa for a little while.

Later Bertha took Wally outside to help him with his reader. She needed something to do to take her mind off of Pa's angry outburst. She decided to write a note to William and Rosa. After several attempts, she tried to explain about Pa and that they wouldn't be seeing her for a while. At least she hoped it would be only for a short while.

Almost in a whisper, she asked, "Wally, do you know where Rosa and William live?"

"Sure, I know where almost everyone in town lives, except a few that moved over to Dennison. Why do you ask?"

"If I ask you to do something, can you keep it a secret? I mean a real honest-to-goodness secret," Bertha whispered.

"Sure, I know how to keep secrets if I have to."

Pleading, she says, "Well, this is a very important secret. Can I trust you to do it?"

By now, Wally was squirming with interest. "What's so important?"

"I have a little note that I want you to take over to Rosa's house and make sure it's her that reads it. No one else." Pausing, she adds, "Well, maybe William could read it, but he probably won't be home."

"Is William your boyfriend? Are you sending him a love note?"

"No, he's not my boyfriend, and it's not a love note. Just skedaddle over and don't tell one single person that I had you do this. Promise? I'm going to tell Ma that you went to see if the big boys are playing brass ball at the water though if she asks where you are. Can you remember that's what we will say if anyone asks?" "I can run over to Rosa's and be back before anyone even misses me," Wally boasted.

As she watched Wally run off, Bertha felt guilty asking Wally to lie for her. *Well, we haven't lied yet, 'cause no one has asked what we are doing. If Ma will just not wonder where Wally is for a few minutes, the message can be delivered.* .

Looking up after a few minutes, she saw Wally running back to the front yard. Amused, she thought that her brother never walks anywhere. He is always running just like a race horse.

He plopped down beside her, grinning and looking around to see if anyone was watching them. Then he sneaked a little piece of paper out of his pocket and put it in Bertha's hand.

She was shocked to see that it said, "Come out your front door at midnight so we can talk."

"Who gave this to you?" she gasped.

"It's from William. He was coming out from his house when I got there, so I gave the note to him. I thought it'd be all right 'cause Rosa wasn't anywhere to be seen. William read the note, and I started to leave, but he called me back, saying to wait, and he went in the house and brought this back to me. What's the matter? Can't he come over?"

"No, Pa doesn't want me to see him anymore, so don't you dare mention this to Pa or Ma either. Promise?"

"I promise, but what does it say?"

"Oh, it's just things you wouldn't understand."

It was getting dark, and Pa had not gotten home yet. Bertha could see that Ma was fretting about him, but neither one said a word.

"I'm kinda feeling poorly, Ma, and I think I'll go to bed early."

"That's a good idea. I think I'll get your brothers ready for bed, and I'll go too."

Bertha lay in bed, wide awake. She heard Pa come home and wondered if he and Ma were talking. Unless Pa's mind got changed, there wasn't much of a reason to try to talk to him. Tears started running down her cheek. She kept thinking about everything that had happened that day.

*Bong, bong, bong*, went the old clock in the parlor. Eleven times it went *bong*. Bertha had heard that clock chime all of her life, but tonight it was different. Every time it went *bong*, her heart went *bong* right along with it. *Do I really have the nerve to sneak out the front door at midnight and meet William, like the note ask me to*? But if she didn't go tonight, how would she ever get to explain things to him. Just one more hour and she could slip out the door. *Oh no, what if the front door squeaks?* She had never even paid any attention to the front door before tonight, so she really didn't know if it squeaked or not. Bertha's chest was getting tight, just thinking about what she was about to do, and she found herself having a hard time breathing.

A squeak could wake up her parents, and then she'd have a terrible time trying to explain what she was doing. *I told Ma that I didn't feel good, so I guess I could always say I was going to be sick to my stomach and needed to get outside. That's really true. I am sick.* If they saw William, I'd have a hard time explaining what he was doing, standing right there at midnight. Slipping out of bed slowly so not to let the brothers hear her and inching to the door, she thought, *So far, so good.* Putting her hand on the door knob, it turned easy with no noise. *The moon is very bright tonight. What if someone sees me?* But probably not too many people were walking around in the middle of the night in Liberal. Slowly going down the steps, she was shocked and also relieved to see William, standing there by the steps, sheepishly grinning at her. She wondered if he could hear her heart pounding.

"I have never in my whole life done anything like this before. I'm really scared."

"I know," he said, grabbing her hand and pulling her close to him, "but we need to talk."

Bertha tried to tell him what was happening in her home, but how could she explain about Pa, when she didn't understand what his thinking was herself?

"I really like you and want us to be together," he whispered and pulled her close. "Do you want that too?"

Words wouldn't come out of her mouth. Being so nervous, she nodded her head yes, which was all she could do. It felt like her heart was going to pound right out of her chest.

"I'd better get back in the house before someone sees us."

Giving her a little hug and a peck on the cheek, he said, "We'll find a way. Don't you be worrying. Just pray for your pa."

"That's what Ma and I did," she whimpered.

"Get your Bible out tomorrow and read Proverbs 3, where is says to *trust in the Lord with all of your heart.* That's what we have to do. Meet me here again tomorrow night, and let me know if your pa has changed his thinking."

Bertha lay in bed, smiling to herself. *Did I really meet William, or did I just dream it?* She knew it wasn't a dream, but it felt like one. Seeing him made the trouble with Pa not seem so terrible, but they couldn't go on meeting at midnight forever, hiding behind the lilac bush.

The Bouton family gathered at the breakfast table as usual, with the boys clamoring for food and Ma busy filling everyone's plates with hoe cakes. Pa acted like his same happy self, but Bertha could feel a lot of tension in the room.

"Tonight, we will be going to a debate at the Mental Liberty Hall," James announced.

Mary and Bertha just put their heads down, not daring to even look at James. *He's trying to change our minds about Jesus*, they both thought.

Wally was excited to be going somewhere. "What's the debate about tonight?"

"Well, I don't rightly know, but you can be sure it will be something that will make us come home and do some deep thinking. Everyone get your good clothes on right after supper, and we'll get there early so we can get a good seat."

Bertha knew what her pa was thinking, but there wasn't any use trying to talk him out of it. His mind was made up, so it looks like they'll be going. Silently, she asked, *Pa, do you really think Harry will sit still? Do you really think I'm going to change my way of thinking?*

---

Everyone loaded up in the wagon and headed to the Mental Liberty Hall, with James trying to make it sound like they were going to a big party. Bertha had already decided that her body would be there, but her mind was going to be somewhere else. The speaker got up and announced that the topic would be a discussion and explanation on the difference between freethinking and free love. Seems like people were getting the idea that it was a free-love, free everything town, which the debater said it definitely was not.

James got a very miserable look on his face, and Mary gave him a look that almost made Bertha giggle to herself. *Pa, I bet you wished we were home.*

After a lot of talk, talk, talk, someone said that they didn't think anyone in the room really believed in free love, but if they did, they should stand up. The speaker was shocked to see a few people stand up. One of those standing was Sam Suydam. Sitting next to Bertha was Sam's mother, who jumped up, crying out loudly, "Oh Sammy, I can't believe you think that awful way." Sam looked like he wished he could fall through the floor, the speaker looked like he wished he was home, and poor ole Mrs. Suydam gasped and fell back in her chair, fanning herself. Several of her friends came to her rescue, and all of a sudden, the meeting was over.

James couldn't think of much to say on the way home, but Wally had lots of questions.

"Wonder why ole Mrs. Suydam got so upset 'cause her boy loved folks? I love all of you, and I sure don't charge for loving you either, 'cause my love's free," Wally declared. "Why'd everyone get all upset?"

Mary gave James a fiery look, and it was all Bertha could do to keep from laughing right out loud. The evening sure didn't go like her pa had planned for it to go.

"Pa, what were they talking about when they said free love?

"Wally, just be still, and someday you and I will have a little talk about things boys need to know, but not tonight."

Not one more word was said all the way home, and everyone went right to bed very quickly.

Bertha was anxious to meet William again and tell him about the meeting. However, it was sort of an embarrassing subject, so she might not be able to tell him about it. She lay still in her bed, anxious to hear the clock strike midnight. A short time was all that she could spend with William. It was just too scary to be out there with him, all alone in the middle of the night.

After telling him about going to the debate, she rushed back into the house, leaped into her bed, and covered herself up with Ma's soft comforter. Just like the night before, it seemed like a dream that she'd been with William. *I have actually been alone with William Fast two nights in a row.*

Next morning, Pa didn't even act like last night was not a very good evening. He called everyone together and announced, "I have great news. Ma and you youngins are going to get on the train tomorrow and go to Pleasant Hill to visit your family up there."

Wally and Harry started jumping all over the kitchen, shouting about a train ride. Bertha had never seen them so happy, but she sure didn't feel like shouting at the news. Mary tried to smile a little and murmured that it'd be good to see her family, but Bertha wondered if Ma was really happy about the trip. Now she wouldn't get to see William for a long time, but maybe she could write him a real letter while she was gone.

---

The day went very quickly, with Mary and Bertha washing and packing clothes for the trip. It was good that everyone was worn out from working and went to bed early. *This would be the last night I will get to see William for a long time. Just when we started liking each other, everything goes wrong.* She quickly slipped out the door, again at midnight. He was waiting for her, and Bertha told him about the trip that they would be taking.

"If Ma will let me, I'll try to write you a letter and let you know about the trip. Now I must say good-bye," she whispered as she quietly went back into her house.

---

Morning seemed to come quickly. James loaded up his family in the wagon very early so there wasn't any chance of them missing the train. It almost seemed like he wanted to get rid of them. *I suppose he thinks I'll forget all about William while I'm gone.*

The feuding in Liberal was even down at the depot. People were there, holding up signs, telling the passengers, who were getting off the train, to just get back on the train if they were Christians. Bertha saw her ma looking at those signs and then gave James a really sad look. Her pa seemed to look the other way and pretended that he didn't even see the signs.

Pa hugged everyone and acted like he had never been angry just a few days ago. As they were getting on the train, Bertha happened to look over at the side of the depot, and there stood William, waving to her. Tears welled from her eyes, but she was able to give him a quick smile before she stepped into the train. Looking out the window, they were able to get one more glimpse of each other as the train rolled away. They were both sad to think it could be a long time before they saw each other again.

James walked back to the wagon, and there was Roberts and Van Camp standing beside it. He quickly pulled them around to the other side of the wagon, hoping that Mary was not watching from the window. Shifting his eyes to the train, he wanted it to pull out of the station before his family looked out the window and saw who he was talking to. *Oh well, it's too late now.* As all three climbed into the wagon, he looked at his two buddies, smiling.

"All right, fellows, we have three weeks to complete our plans. Let's get busy."

# Chapter 5

*Click, click, click.* Every time Bertha heard that noise from the train wheels, it just reminded her she was going a little farther from William. Her insides were all mixed up, feeling sad to leave yet happy to be visiting her grandparents. Looking over at her brothers, she was really glad that they were gazing at everything they could catch a glimpse of as the train rumbled through the countryside. The engine kept belching big puffs of smoke, and soot was covering their good clothes. Glancing over at her ma, she looked completely worn out.

"Just lay your head back and take a nap. I'll watch the boys for you."

"I'm all right. When we get to Grandpa and Grandma's place, I'll rest then. They'll entertain the boys for days."

"I hate to say this, Ma, but it seemed to me that Pa was really anxious for us to go on this trip. It was almost like he wanted to get rid of us for some reason. Do you think it was because of William?"

"No, he bought the train fares before he told you he didn't want William to be coming around. He even let Grandpa know we were coming before he told me about the trip.

It did seem like he was wanting us to go real strongly, but I think he just wanted to surprise us with something good. He knows that we all miss our family up at Pleasant Hill."

"Why don't we ever hear anything about Pa's family? I never hear him talk about his folks. Is he an orphan?"

Shrugging her shoulders, she answered, "I don't really know much. All I know is your pa won't talk about his relatives, but I do know he moved to Missouri from the East Coast."

"The East Coast!" Bertha exclaimed. "That's a long ways from Missouri."

"He and his family had some kind of feud, and he just walked away from them and has never looked back. In fact, he changed his last name. A long time ago he started calling himself Bouton. I've wondered about his family too, but that's all he ever told me."

"Pa sure must have been really angry to even change his name. It's too bad we don't know them, but maybe they aren't good people."

"I think the feud had something to do with Christianity. You saw how upset he was when we came home from the preaching. It must have brought back some old memories."

"Maybe that's why he likes Mr. Walser. They both are rejecting Christianity."

"That could be true. We need to keep praying for your pa and Mr. Walser too."

Bertha abruptly changed the subject, thinking this was a good time to ask a question.

"Can I write William a letter while we're gone? I really want to explain some things to him. Pa didn't say I couldn't write to him, just said not to see him."

"Let me think about it awhile. Right now I just want to relax and forget all about what's been happening in our home and in Liberal."

"I won't ask any more today, but I'm sure hoping you'll say yes tomorrow. You know I really like William a whole lot, don't you?"

---

The days passed quickly at Pleasant Hill, with Grandpa and Grandma and all the other family members planning fun things every day. Mary decided to let Bertha write one letter to William. He did deserve some explanation about James's strange behavior, she thought. But how could anyone really explain his behavior? He was acting very strange indeed.

A letter soon arrived from James, and Mary gathered the family together to listen it to.

*Dear Family*

*I trust that you are all enjoying the visit with your family. I'm keeping very busy so I won't miss you so much. I've made a few changes in my doctoring room.*

*Mary, I want you to start instructing the children to not go into that room.*

*If you keep reminding them of that every day, when you get home, they will, hopefully, remember it.*

*Our town is becoming quite a beautiful place since Mr. Walser and his friends have been busy planting catalpa trees all along Main Street.*

*He is also creating a lovely park down south of Main Street, calling it Catalpa Park. Close to the park, he is building a beautiful home, and I understand that about $40,000 is being spent on these projects.*

*Some of the streets in Liberal are getting names of rather famous men-Darwin, Ingersoll, and Fishback being three of them. These men have become well-known for their lively debates, and Mr. Walser admires their thinking and their intellect.*

*The Guffys and other spirited citizens have been instrumental in a large bell being installed at the northeast corner of the city park. This bell has been placed on some large blocks, brought in from the Curless stone quarry. When rung, it has an extremely loud tone, which will arouse people, either day or night, alerting the fire brigade and surely saving homes and businesses from being destroyed by fire.*

*These improvements is making Liberal a better community. I am expecting visitors to start coming to our home in the coming days, but I don't want you to fret about them causing you extra work. It is private types of meetings, and they will be staying at Walser's Ozark Hotel. They won't bother you at all.*

*I am looking forward to your return home and will be at the depot, awaiting your arrival.*

*Giving my best regards to your family and my love to you, I remain, your husband and father, James B. Bouton*

Every one sat quietly, thinking about James's letter, except Wally, who was always the first to talk about any subject.

"Pa sure does like to talk about all the good things that are going on in Liberal, doesn't he?"

"Yes, Wally, your pa is right fond of Liberal," Mary stated wearily. "Now you and Harry can go back to your playing since you've heard Pa's letter."

"James does write a right pleasing letter, I'll have to agree," Grandpa Claude added. "He always was good with words."

"Yes, but the words he didn't mention was about all the feuding that's going on down there. Now that Walser has built that fence, there's no telling what's going to happen next," Mary snapped.

Thinking out loud, Bertha murmured, "Pa's hoping that fence will keep William and me apart, but we're praying it won't."

Since Bertha was usually shy and quiet, the family was almost shocked when she spoke. Grandma reached over, gave her a big hug, saying, "Don't you be fretting, honey, 'cause this family believes in prayer, and we'll just keep praying for your pa. God will soften his heart. Just be patient."

Tears started to run down her face, and she jumped up, embarrassed for speaking what was in her heart, and ran out of the parlor, into the bedroom.

Breaking the silence, Grandpa declared, "Even if she is my granddaughter, and I ought not to brag on her, she's a good girl. I sure hate to see James causing her so much sadness."

---

A few days later, Grandpa Claude came in the house, waving a letter, smiling at Bertha.

"Just look what I got in the mail today. Do you suppose it's a love letter?" he teased.

Quick as a flash, she bolted out of the chair, knowing it was a letter from William.

Grabbing the letter, she ran into the other room. They all laughed as grandma announced, "Well, it doesn't look like we'll be getting to hear what that letter says, does it?"

Coming back into the room later, Bertha's face was bright, with a huge smile from ear to ear. "William says he misses me and that things are about the same in Liberal. Several businesses are moving to Pedro, and the fence is causing a lot of talk all over the whole country. Newspapers from just everywhere are writing about it."

Speaking sharply, Mary answered, "One of these days, Liberal's going to be a ghost town if things don't settle down. Then they can write about that."

Agreeing, her mother commented, "There's no telling what some of those ruffians will do. I just pray that no one will be hurt or maybe even killed. This fussing could lead to bloodshed."

---

Tucking the letter into her apron pocket, Bertha took it out and read it several times that day. She was trying to help her grandma with some cooking chores, but it was hard to think of anything else. *Can't Pa see that William's a good fellow? I'd think he'd rather me like a good Christian man than some old drunk that was hanging out at that new saloon in Pedro.* As she and Grandma peeled taters for supper, she sort of whispered to herself and to grandma, "It's just not fair for Pa to say that William was putting foolishness in my mind."

Giving her a big squeeze, Grandma said, "I know, darling, but remember that Proverbs says to trust in the Lord with all your heart and lean not to your own understanding."

Just then, Wally came running in, yelling that Harry was hurt. Everyone rushed to the screaming little fellow as Wally shouted, "He dun went and stepped on a big ole nail, and his foot is having a whole lot of bleed coming out of it."

Grandpa grabbed him up in his big arms, using a rag to press against his little foot, and the bleeding soon stopped.

Wishfully, Mary said, "If James had only come along; he'd have something to put on it."

Grandma wiped Harry's face, drying the tears with her old worn apron. "Go get a piece of fat from that hog jowls, and we'll put it on his little foot. If any poison from that nail tries to go in his foot, that fat'll draw it out."

---

The three-week visit quickly came to an end, so Mary and her children had to bid farewell to the family. After many hugs, tears, and kisses, they climbed aboard the train for that long trip back to Liberal. Harry and Wally were very tired from all the activities at their grandparents' house, so the swaying back and forth quickly put them to sleep.

Finally speaking, Bertha asked, "What do you think Pa meant in his letter when he said visitors would be coming past?"

"I've been wondering that myself. He was sort mysterious about it, wasn't he?"

"The only visitor I want to come past is William." Bertha sighed. "He said in his letter he likes me a lot."

"Yes, I know, but your pa wants you to go to the college and meet a few more boys. You're really too young to decide on a bow just now."

"I don't care beans about that college. Those teachers think like Walser does and I've got my own thoughts about freethinking. It's just the opposite of Walser's thinking too.

Finally the train chugged into Liberal, whistling its arrival. Everyone was looking out windows, anxious to get off and stretch their legs.

"There's Pa, waving at us," Wally shouted.

James was waving and had a huge smile on his face. Anyone could tell that just seeing his family again was making him real happy. After lots of hugs for everyone, he loaded their trunk in the wagon, and they started down the street to their house. All of a sudden, he got rather stern and started questioning Mary as to whether she had instructed the children as to what he'd written about them no longer going into his doctoring room.

Gruffly spitting the words out and looking at the children, he said, "This room is now private, and you are not allowed to ever go in there again. Do you all understand?"

This was a subject Mary was eager to talk to him about, along with the news that visitors were coming past, but she'd decided to wait till the children were in bed for that discussion. However, since he had brought up the subject, she decided it was time for the talk.

"Land's sake, James, what's so private about that room? The boys have never bothered anything in there, have they?"

"Well, no, but just make sure they don't go in there."

Deciding to face the other subject right then, she continued, "What did you mean about visitors starting to come past the house? Who will it be and what do they want anyway?"

"Oh, people from out of town and a few local folks will probably be coming past some evenings. I'm having some meetings in my room sometimes. You won't even know that they're around."

"What kind of meetings are you talking about?" Mary demanded.

Speaking so softly that it was almost impossible to hear, he said, "Well, I'm having spiritualist meetings."

Unable to hold her anger and not even thinking about the children in the back of the wagon, she said, "James Bouton, do you mean to tell me you're taking up that tomfoolery that Walser does, like talking to the dead?"

"Now dear, it's not anything to cause you to fret. You and the children won't even know whose stopping past for a meeting."

The three children all sat still as mice, listening to their parents' arguing.

This was something they rarely ever heard. It was almost frightening, and they knew it was a time for them to be very silent.

"I've fixed my room so it will be private, and you won't be bothered at all."

Everyone was silent, with the mule's *clop, clop, clopping* being the only noise to be heard. As the wagon rounded the corner, headed toward the Bouton home, Wally couldn't be still any longer.

"Look, Ma, there's a new door in our house. It goes right into Pa's doctoring room."

Staring in astonishment, they all saw that their home now had two doors in the front. One new door went into the doctor's room, and the old one, which went into the parlor, was still there.

Looking at her husband with tears in her eyes, Mary said, "Well, I guess this explains why you sent us to Pleasant Hill for three weeks. You've taken up company with the devil."

# Chapter 6

THE FIRST DAY BACK home was a very quiet day. Harry and Wally were happy to be back in their own house and kept busy, playing with the new wooden toys their grandpa Claude had made them. James enjoyed watching them zoom the little toys back and forth over the floor. Once in a while, thoughts of his father jumped into his mind. *Wonder what kind of grandfather he'd be? These boys will never know their other grandfather, but at least Mary's parents are wonderful to my children.*

James told the family that their Ma was tired and feeling poorly, so Bertha unpacked their clothes and tried to keep the boys quiet, letting her ma rest. However, every time she peeked inside their bedroom, Ma was reading her Bible.

Finally, the family gathered together for the evening meal, and Pa was trying to be very cheerful.

Smiling at the boys, he said, "Well, tell me all about the fun you had up at grandpa and grandma's house!"

After thinking only a second, Wally bounced around, waving his hands. "I went fishing and caught a fish this long. Harry caught one too, didn't you?"

"Yes, me caught a big fish," Harry declared.

Mary and Bertha were silent, letting James and the boys carry on the conversation.

It was plain to see that James was trying to get everyone in a good mood that evening.

"Since you boys know how to catch fish, we'll go fishing someday soon, and you can show me how to catch a big fish. How does that sound?"

Both boys clapped their hands in excitement. "When will that be, Pa? Where will we go catch those big fish?"

"Oh, I think we might go to Nickerson's Creek out west of town, but fishermen will probably get really hungry so we need to get your ma and Bertha to make us lunch. We'll load up in the wagon one day soon and try our luck at fishing.

Continuing, he said, "In fact, I think it'd be great fun if Ma and Bertha came along, don't you?"

Mary could see that James was trying hard to bring her into his plans to keep the family happy, but she never said a word in reply. However, Bertha quickly thought this would probably be a good time to ask her pa a difficult question.

"Pa, I think going fishing would be lots of fun, but I'd have a lot more fun if I could ask my good friend Rosa Fast to come along with us. Would that be all right?"

James got an unhappy look on his face for a short second, and Mary hid a little smile from him, glancing at Bertha.

Almost amused, she thought, *This is the perfect time, Bertha, to talk about the Fasts since he's trying to be so nice. He may say yes to anything.*

"Yes, you probably would have a good time showing Rosa how to catch fish, so she will be welcome to go along. You and your ma start planning what good food you will be fixing to take along, and we'll have a real special day soon."

Later, James went outside to do his evening chores, and Bertha remarked to her ma, "You can sure tell that Pa is trying to make us all happy and not be mad about his meetings in the doctoring room, can't you?"

"Well, it's going to take more than a fishing trip to get me to accept what he's going to be doing in there. I've got some Bible words to be showing him about what God has to say regarding these kinds of things. He may not like to hear what I've got to say, but for once, I'm saying what needs to be said."

"What does the Bible say?"

"I've been studying on it, and in Deuteronomy it says that anyone who is a medium or spiritualist or consults the dead is detestable to the Lord."

"Oh dear, that is really scary."

Just then, James came back into the room, and they both were silent.

"Bertha, I forgot to mention that Mrs. Guffy wanted you to come to her house and help with some chores. She's been poorly lately and has a hard time keeping her housework done. If it's all right with your ma, I'll take you down there in the morning." Walking over to his wife and giving her a hug, he added, "In fact, why don't I take the boys along with us for a little ride, and you can have the morning completely to yourself. Just relax and do whatever you want to in the morning."

"If I can get Mrs. Guffy's work done in the morning, I'll come back home and help you in the afternoon, Ma."

"That's fine. Just help her as long as she needs you."

---

The Bouton boys were excited to get to spend time with their pa, going for a buggy ride around town, and Bertha was happy to go to Mrs. Guffy's to work. Pa was trying to be extra nice to everyone, and Ma was glad to be alone for a little while.

"Don't try to come back and pick me up, Pa. I'll be glad to walk home when we get our work done." As the buggy drove away, she was thinking that today would be the perfect time to walk past Rosa's house on her way home. Pa did say she could invite her to go fishing, and how would she know about the outing if she didn't stop past to tell her about it. Smiling to herself, she thought, *I sure hope William is home.*

---

Working for the Guffys went very quickly, because Bertha kept thinking of going past the Fasts' house as she walked to her home. It was almost as if Rosa had been watching for her to come past. As she got close to the Fasts, their door flew open, and Rosa came leaping out, running to greet Bertha.

She shouted, "When did you get back to Liberal? Does your Pa know you're coming past? I sure wish William was home to see you."

Hugging her friend, she answered, "Yes, Pa said I could invite you to go fishing with us some time."

"If this doesn't beat all. Does this mean you can start to see William again and go to church with us?"

"Well, I'm not so sure. I didn't have the nerve to ask Pa that. I just said I wanted to take you on our family outing, and he said it would be all right."

Bertha was quiet for a few seconds, wondering if she should confide in her friend about the meetings her pa was planning to have. She was very embarrassed to even think about his plans, let alone tell them to Rosa.

"I'm so glad you came past. I heard Mama and Papa talking about something they heard up town about your pa. I'm not sure I should be telling you, but it seems like it's something you ought to know."

Dropping her head down so Rosa couldn't see the hurt in her eyes, she said, "I already know what you are talking about. Its meetings Pa is having, isn't it?"

"Yes, land's sakes, what is he thinking about?"

"That's what Ma and I are wondering too."

"I guess he's putting out a pamphlet about speaking to the dead, and some folks are real excited about doing just that very thing. In fact, I think maybe he had a few meetings while you folks were gone."

"Pa is really trying to be nice to us and make us happy, but it's causing trouble between him and Ma. That, I can tell for sure. Ma and Grandma said we just have to keep praying for him."

Bertha was sad to learn that William was not home, and she told Rosa that she didn't know when they could see each other again.

"Do you think he will even want to see me again, with all of this spiritualist stuff going on in my very own home?"

"It's not your fault your Pa wants to do that. William knows that it's not your idea."

After enjoying a good visit, Bertha started walking on to her house, having to go a few extra blocks to get around the fence that Walser put up. Each step made her more upset with her pa's ideas and with Walser's ideas too.

*I'd like to go back to Grandma and Grandma's and just live there. But I'd want William to live there too.*

As she came nearer her home, Wally and Harry saw her coming and ran to meet her.

"Guess what Pa bought us? We got candy."

Bertha smiled at her brothers and thought to herself, *Well, it looks like a piece of candy has got the boys on Pa's side.*

Meeting her daughter at the door, Mary Bouton had a grim look on her face.

"Well, we will be spending tonight in the back room, 'cause your pa is having one of those meetings in his room. I just don't understand him. One minute he is trying to have a good time with us, and the next minute, he's all worked up about having people come to call up the dead."

"Did you talk to him about what the Bible says about that kind of stuff?"

"Oh yes, but it was like talking to a tree stump. I don't think he even heard me. I could tell his mind was a thousand miles away."

"I went past Rosa's house to invite her to the fishing trip, and she said she thinks maybe he has already had some meetings while we were gone."

"Yes, I think he has. He said that sometime, you and I could go in and watch what they do. But I don't think I want any part of that, do you?"

"No, let's just fix bread and jam for the boys, get some books, and take them in the back room and try to pretend we're having a little picnic."

Lighting the lamp, taking it and her children to the back room, Mary felt like a black cloud was hovering over their house. James has invited the devil himself to come in, and there wasn't anything she could do about it.

Mary and Bertha played like it was a little game to be reading books to the boys and eating in the back room, instead of at the kitchen table.

The Bouton boys soon fell asleep, but Mary and Bertha listened as doors opened and shut. They just stared at each other as they heard soft voices coming from Pa's room.

After a while, curiosity got the best of Mary. "You stay here with the boys so I can go out front and look in the window and see what's going on."

"Oh, Ma, be careful. You've heard that curiosity killed the cat."

"Well, this is our house too, and I want to know what kind of goings-on your pa is bringing in this home."

The only sound Bertha heard was the deep snoring of her brothers. It seemed like her ma was gone forever when the door opened.

Coming in the room with a puzzled look on her face, she said, "I know there's folks in that room, because two buggies are parked out in front … don't recognize either of them. The windows are covered with something dark and I can't see in the room at all."

"What did you hear?"

"Not one thing, no sound at all was coming from the room."

Shaking with fright, Bertha whispered, "Makes a body feel real creepy."

"Yes, it makes me very uncomfortable to think it's going on in our home. And I felt really foolish trying to peek in my own window."

"I feel like we don't really know Pa sometimes. It's like someone else is stepping into his mind and his body."

Nodding, she agreed, "We might as well try to get some sleep. Doesn't look like your pa will be coming to bed for a while."

---

It was again a tense morning at the Bouton breakfast table. James never came to their bedroom, and Mary never asked where he slept. He was very quiet, not trying to get the family in a jolly mood this morning, like he had on previous mornings.

Dishing up eggs to everyone, Mary said, "Wally, I'll be needing some more eggs fetched in before noon."

"What you makin'?"

"Oh, I thought I'd make a custard dessert like Grandma Pearl made for you."

"Oh boy," he said, looking at his father. "Pa, if you'd gone with us to Grandma's, you'd sure like to have tasted her new custard dessert. I ate a whole bunch of it. Didn't I, Ma?"

Speaking almost without an emotion, she answered, "Yes, I'm sure he would have enjoyed Grandma's cooking."

James quickly finished his breakfast and went outside. You could tell he had a lot on his mind besides hearing his children's chatter.

Mary and Bertha were both nervous while cleaning up the kitchen and hardly said a word to each other. Mary kept glancing out the window, watching James as he went about doing his morning chores. Later, James Roberts and W. S. Van Camp walked into the yard, and they all went over behind the shed. Somehow, Mary was not at all surprised to see them coming past again.

"There's Roberts and Van Camp again," she complained to her daughter.

"I knew those scalawags and James were up to something, even before we left for Pleasant Hill."

"Do you think they help Pa with his meetings?"

"Yes, they are probably part of whatever he is doing."

"If Grandpa and Grandma knew what Pa was doing right in our own house, I'll bet they'd want us to come back and stay with them, wouldn't they?

"Yes, I'm sure they would."

"Are you going to write and tell them about it?"

"No, not yet. I'll just write and say to keep praying for your pa."

# Chapter 7

TIME PASSED SLOWLY FOR Bertha and Mary. The séances continued night after night, much to their displeasure. James seemed to be living in another world, far apart from his family. He was constantly rushing off somewhere, not telling anyone where he was going or when he would come home. Robert and Van Camp stopped by almost every day for private visits in the backyard.

Mary called to her daughter, "I need some groceries from town. I'll make a list, and you go get these things for me."

"Oh Ma, I just can't go," Bertha whimpered. "The last time I was in Browns, I heard some folks whispering about Pa's meetings. They didn't think I could hear them, but I sure did. I didn't want to tell you, but Rosa says everyone is talking about Pa's meetings."

Mary walked over and gave Bertha a hug. "I'd hoped you hadn't heard all the gossip that's going around town. I heard the same thing the last time I went to Brown's."

"What are we going to do, Ma?"

Mary was quiet for a minute. "Well, first I'm telling James that we won't be going to town, so he can do the trading for us."

"Have you written Grandma and Grandpa about what's happening with Pa's meetings?"

Mary shook her head. "No, but they want to come visit us. When I tell your pa they want to come see us, he keeps saying for me to tell them to wait a few weeks. He knows my father would be mad and take us all back to Pleasant Hill if he saw what was going on in our home."

"Well, if I wouldn't miss William, I'd like to leave Liberal today and never come back. These meetings are scaring me every night."

The next morning at breakfast, James was smiling and said he had some good news to tell the family. Mary and Bertha looked at each other, both hoping he was going to say the spiritualist meetings were over. However, that was not the news.

"A man named Henry Wiggins is traveling from New York to Liberal, and he has invited all of us to join him for a meal at the Ozark Hotel tomorrow."

Looking at Mary, he asked, "Won't that be a treat to go down to the hotel and let their cooks fix our meal? You won't have to work at all."

Turning to the boys, he said, "Now boys, I'm expecting you to be on your best behavior when we go to the hotel. Is that understood?"

Harry and Wally smiled at their pa. "Will we be eating in the fancy dining room that I heard Mr. Brown talking about?" Wally asked.

"Yes, I imagine we'll be in that room. Mr. Walser will be joining us. Your ma will be getting our good clothes ready for us to wear. We'll all have a wonderful time. Just behave yourself and make me proud of you," he said as he rushed out the door as usual.

Mary muttered almost to herself, "I wish James would behave himself and make us proud of him."

"What do you think that Mr. Wiggins is coming to Liberal for, Ma?"

"Beats me. I'll try to ask your pa more about it tonight, but he is hard to catch for any visiting since he started these meetings."

"I know. He hardly knows we're even here anymore. I'm praying these meetings will stop, aren't you?"

"Yes, the quicker they stop, the better off we will be for sure."

"Ma, is it all right if I go down to Rosa's house for a little while? She and William are the only people I can talk to about Pa's meetings. They aren't laughing behind my back about them."

"Yes, go on. Your pa has completely forgotten about wanting you to stop seeing them."

"I won't be gone long. Just seems like I need to get away from this spooky place."

"I know." Mary sighed. "I know what you mean."

---

The Bouton family was up early, dressed in their finest clothes and ready to go down town to the Ozark Hotel. James kept mentioning how lucky they were to be invited to dine with Mr. Wiggins and Mr. Walser. Mary and Bertha just looked at each other, knowing they had different thought on the subject.

As they rode down the street in their wagon, Wally was chattering as usual. "Guess what Tommy told me, Pa? He said you had a church in our house."

Mary gave James a startled look, waiting for him to answer Wally.

"Now Wally," James replied, "I think you know I do not have a church in our house. Just tell Tommy he doesn't know what he is talking about."

"But, Pa, he even told me the name of the church. Said it was The Church of the Icy Hand. Said they meet right in your doctoring room."

Mary looked like she was about to faint and fall off of the wagon. She put her hands over her face and said, "Oh James, look what you have done to this family."

"Now, we're not going to let some boy's silly talk ruin our party today. Just forget about this nonsense and think about what we will soon be eating. No more questions, Wally. Just be quiet."

As the wagon pulled up to the hotel, Mary and Bertha looked like they were going to a funeral, not a fancy dinner party. Mr. Walser and an elderly man were standing on the porch, smiling and waving at them. James waved back as he helped his family down from the wagon and introduced them to Mr. Wiggins. Mary grabbed Harry's hand and Bertha grabbed Wally, and they all marched into the hotel.

During the meal, Mr. Wiggins wanted to keep talking about his dear departed mother.

"Bless her soul," he kept saying. "I feel my dear mother has a message for me."

Mary and Bertha kept their heads down, looking at their plates and not talking at all.

James was soon able to steer the conversation away from Mr. Wiggins' mother and started talking about the Liberal Free Thought University. He mentioned to everyone that he wanted to enroll Bertha in it soon. That pleased Mr. Walser and Mr. Wiggins, but it sure made a big lump come up in Bertha's throat. She wanted to get up and run out the door but knew she couldn't. Just then, the waitress brought a big cake to the table, and everyone started talking about how delicious it looked.

Wally had kept quiet as long as possible and finally asked, "Mr. Wiggins, is there lots of people in New York City?"

"Yes, Wally, there's lots of people coming from all over the world to live in America, and they usually start out in New York."

Wally was watching Mr. Wiggins and taking in every word he spoke. "Gosh, I'd like to see New York, wouldn't you, Pa?"

Mr. Wiggins was happy to talk about New York. "Just last month there was a huge number of people right in front of my business, watching a parade go past, and guess who was in the parade?"

Wally was sitting on the edge of his seat, waiting for the story to go on.

"It was our president, Grover Cleveland, riding right past my office in a fine carriage."

"Really? You saw the president? Boy, I wish I could see the president."

James finally pulled Wally back in his seat. "Let Mr. Wiggins finish his dessert so we can be leaving this fine establishment."

On the way home, Wally was the only one that seemed to be excited about the trip to the hotel. "Boy, Ma, wasn't that good cake? I wish we could have that every day, don't you?"

"Yes, Wally the cake was good," Mary slowly replied. It was clear she had something else on her mind. Then turning to James, she asked, "What did Mr. Wiggins mean when he said he would see us tonight?"

"Well, he wants to come over to my meeting tonight. But don't you be fretting. You and the children will be in the back room and won't be disturbed at all."

Mary raised her voice. "James, we're getting tired of being stuck in the back room every night. We feel like we're hiding from something."

"Now, Mary, you and the children are fine. Let's not be talking this way in front of them.

We'll talk sometime later." He patted her hand and gave her a stern look.

As they pulled up to the yard, Mary said, "Bertha, take the boys inside and get their good clothes off. Your pa and I need to talk privately."

Bertha was happy to take the boys in the house 'cause it was time that Ma had her say to her pa. *Maybe this time Pa will listen to her.*

Mary came in later with tears in her eyes.

"Ma, did it do any good to talk to Pa?" Bertha whispered.

"No, I don't think he paid any attention at all. I told him we are afraid in our own home, and he just said to not fret about it. That's all he ever says—'just don't fret.'"

Mary went in the back room for a while. When she came back out, she had a determined look on her face. "Tonight I'm going into James meeting and find out what is really happening in that room."

"Oh, Ma, I'll be scared without you in the back room with me and the boys. Don't go."

"I need to know what's going on, and there's only one way to find out. When your pa goes in there, I'm going in too. I don't think he'll make a big fuss about me being there in front of Mr. Wiggins."

"All right, Ma, I guess I'll keep the boys quiet and be praying all the time you are in there."

Later, after dark, Mary heard voices in James's room, and she just walked right through the door that they were never supposed to enter. When her ma didn't come right back out, Bertha decided she must be staying. She took her brothers to the back room to spend the evening reading and playing games. Finally they all fell asleep. Mary peeked in later and told Bertha she would visit with her in the morning.

The Bouton kitchen was silent, with no one speaking or even looking at each other. Bertha could hardly wait for her pa to go outside so she could ask her ma about the meeting. James quickly ate and went out to do the chores. Bertha pulled her chair close to her ma.

Whispering, she asked, "What happened last night? Was it scary?"

Mary started her recollection of the past evening event in a hushed tone. "Your pa sure didn't want me in the room, but he didn't want to make a fuss in front of Mr. Wiggins, so he got a chair and firmly put me in the corner with a stern look that said 'You sit here and be quiet.' All Mr. Wiggins wanted to do was blab about his dear mother, and James just sat beside him, listening for a long time."

Bertha was full of questions. "What did the room look like? Was it spooky?"

Mary nodded yes. "James has made a little box and put it high up on the wall with a candle in it. Some blue paper covers a hole in the box, so just a little light was shining out into the room."

"Pa needed us to be gone while he did all of this, didn't he?" Bertha interrupted.

Mary agreed. "He has a closet in the corner with a big fancy dark brown velvet drape over it. I've never seen material like it in Liberal. Don't know where he bought it."

"Remember Pa studying the Sears and Roebuck catalogue a lot right before we went to Pleasant Hill? I bet he ordered it, making sure it came after we were gone, don't you?"

"Probably so. Last night showed me there's a lot I don't know about your pa."

"What else happened?"

"Well, James turned the lamp off, and it was so dark we could hardly see. I guess he wanted it that way. Mr. Wiggins kept saying he wanted to know if his dear mother was all right, so James wrote something on a little slate and put it behind that fancy drape. There was a door behind it, and in a few minutes, he would open the drape and door.

"There was the slate with some writing on it. James showed it to Mr. Wiggins, and he was overjoyed. Then we could see a white figure in that closet, and Mr. Wiggins got real happy. He said that was his dear mother 'cause that was the dress she had on before she died. I think he was starting to try to kiss her, but James grabbed him and said, 'Oh no, you can't touch her, we'd lose contact with the spirits."

Bertha gasped. "Oh, were you scared?"

Mary whispered, "Yes, I was, and I'm still shaking."

"Do you think it was his mother coming back to talk to him?"

Mary thought a minute. "Well, I don't know who it was, but Mr. Wiggins sure seemed happy when he left. There was a plate for money, and I'm sure he put some in it. Guess that is where your pa is getting his extra money lately. It was dark in there most of the time except for that spooky light up high. James did light a little lantern to help Mr. Wiggins out the door and to his buggy."

Mary just sat still, trying to think what she needed to say next.

"Are you going back to another meeting?"

"No," Mary declared. "I've seen and heard all I want to see. I'm about ready to tell your pa that we are leaving if he insists on having these meetings in our home. It's not right and I don't want you children to be part of it."

"Well, I guess we aren't really part of it, but it makes me scared to think about.

Do you think Pa likes having these meetings more than he likes us?"

"I certainly hope not, but things are sure different now than what they were when we first came down to Liberal."

They both sat quietly, each thinking their own thoughts.

"I'd sure hate to leave William, but I'll go if you think we should."

"Let's keep praying a few more days, and if your pa keeps having these meetings,

I'm telling him we are going back to Pleasant Hill."

"The boys would sure miss Pa, wouldn't they?"

"Yes, but I don't want him dragging them into this stuff when they get older. No telling what it might do to them."

# Chapter 8

THE CLANGING OF THE fire bell in the city park woke Bertha from a deep sleep.

Jumping out of bed, she ran into the parlor. She almost ran into her parents, who were running to look out the front window.

"Ma, I smell smoke. What do you think is on fire?"

It was almost daylight, and they could see people running in their front yard.

About that time, someone was pounding on the front door, yelling that their house was on fire. James and Mary rushed to grab their boys and practically pushed Bertha out the front door. Here was a group of frantic neighbors, pointing to the roof of their house. Looking up, Bertha could see smoke creeping out from the roof. She was so scared that she just couldn't move, so a neighbor pulled her back, away from the house. By that time, James and Mary came out with the boys, who were both starting to cry. The scene was total confusion until Art Guffy, the fire marshal, climbed on the roof with his ax. He started chopping a hole in the roof, trying to find the source of where the smoke was coming from.

"Oh no!" James called to him. "Don't go in the attic."

Art didn't listen to him and kept right on chopping a hole in the roof. The men of the community started bringing in water for Art to pour in the hole he had just cut in the roof. He then lowered himself down into the hole and soon came out with a big grin on his face. Bertha instantly wondered why anyone would be grinning about a house being on fire. She looked over at James, and he had a terrible look on his face.

She whispered to Mary, "Look at Pa. He looks like he is really frightened. Do you think our house is going to burn down?"

Mary couldn't even answer Bertha. She just pulled her boys close to her and kept praying that the house would not burn down. The boys were crying, and she was busy consoling them but also wondered why in the world a firefighter would be happy to see a house on fire.

"Here's your ghosts, folks," he yelled and held up some white flowing material, waving it down to the people on the ground. "Look what I just found."

The entire group of people stood very still for a few seconds, trying to understand what Art was talking about. He proceeded to hold up a few more objects, waving them in the air, and smiled a big toothy grin. All of the neighbors burst into laughter while they looked at James for an explanation.

It took Mary a second to realize what Art had found. "Oh, James, there is your dead spirits. The joke that you are hiding in our attic has backfired on you," she gasped.

Bertha stood still, looking at her pa, realizing that his spiritual meetings were a big hoax. In a way, she was extremely relieved but also became embarrassed at the way the neighbors were all laughing and pointing at James. *What if they think Ma and I knew about the attic secrets?*

The fire was probably caused by the candle being used for the spooky lighting effects, and it was quickly put out. The people all started to leave but were still having a good laugh over the spiritual meetings.

Mary still was holding on to her boys and grabbed Bertha's arm and led them away from the laughter into the backyard. James just stood still, looking very foolish and not saying a thing.

"Ma, why was Pa fooling the people with all that stuff?" Bertha whispered.

"We don't know what was going on, but it sure looks like his meetings are over.

I'm so embarrassed, but I guess our prayers got answered in a way I never expected."

For once, Wally was very quiet, just standing by his ma, wide-eyed. He kept looking at her for an explanation about what was going on. No one had an explanation, except James. And right now, all he was doing was standing there, looking foolish.

Tears ran down Bertha's face as she whispered, "I was embarrassed about those meetings, and now I'm even more ashamed about Pa's trickery. I don't want to ever look at another person in Liberal again. Let's leave today and go to Pleasant Hill."

"Just wait and see what your pa has to say for himself."

James and several of his buddies kept busy most of the morning, repairing the roof. When they all came in for lunch, Mary quickly set out the food but hardly said a word to anyone. They just ate and went back out to continue their repair work. The house smelled like smoke, so Bertha and Mary opened all of the windows. The boys ran around the rooms, waving little fans, with the idea they were chasing the bad smell outside and enjoying their little game.

Finally, James came in that evening, and Mary just kept quiet, looking at him She was waiting for an explanation, and James knew he was in trouble with her.

He tried to give her and Bertha a little sickly grin and said these meetings were just harmless gatherings. He was just helping some people feel better and was earning extra money so he could buy things for his family. He spoke as if he was trying to convince himself along with convincing Mary and Bertha.

"Bertha and I are so embarrassed that we never want to see another person in this town again. You are not the same man I married. I feel like I don't even know you anymore. I can't live here any longer, so I'm taking the children and going back to Pleasant Hill and live with my family."

James hung his head, knowing that what Mary said was true. He finally reached over and took her hand and said, "Come take a little ride with me in the buggy, and we can talk this over alone."

Mary shook her head. "No, I'll go out in the backyard and talk, but I won't go riding around town like I'm in a parade. These people will be staring at us and laughing for a mighty long time."

"Now Mary, you can't say for sure what people are talking about. You and the children never did one thing wrong. It was me that had this little game going. It was just a little fun and a way to make some money too. You like nice things, don't you?"

Mary didn't say a word, just walked out the back door with James following her like a little puppy. Bertha wondered what in the world her pa could say to her ma that will change Mary's mind about leaving. *He sure is going to have to do a lot of sweet-talking.* A big lump came up in Bertha's throat, and tears were running down her face again. She was torn between leaving Liberal and not being with William or staying and facing all of these people every day. *I guess I'm going to have to pray for peace again.*

Bertha's parents stayed outside for a long time, so she took the boys to bed. *This has been a terrible day, and I feel like I'm going to have a restless night. Wonder what Pa and Ma can be talking about for such a long time.*

Finally, morning came, and Bertha heard her parents in the kitchen. She almost dreaded going in where they were, but she was anxious to find out what was going on.

She finally pulled herself out of bed and headed to the kitchen.

Both parents had pleasant looks on their faces. Ma said, "I have good news for you.

Your Pa is going to the preaching with us tonight."

This news really took Bertha by surprise. She was totally speechless and grabbed a chair before she fell down on the floor. *Is this the same man who was against preaching just a few weeks ago?*

Mary had a slight smile on her face. "Bertha, you will need to help me get our clothes ready for going to the preaching. I don't know if they will smell like smoke or not."

James hurried outside, not wanting to be the center of their conversation.

"Are you sure Pa is really going? Maybe he just said that to keep us here."

"Well, he promised that he would go, so I guess we will see what happens tonight."

"You don't think he will go and cause trouble like Mr. Walser does sometimes? I've heard he tries to disrupt church preaching real often."

"He'd better not do that, or I'll come right home and start packing our clothes and leave tomorrow. I think he knows that he's very close to losing his family, and he seems to want to try to make this right with us. Let's just pray that something will be said at the preaching that will soften his heart."

"Can I run down and tell Rosa that we are going?"

"Yes, I guess it won't hurt for her family to be praying about us going to the preaching."

"People sure will be surprised to see the Bouton family walk into the church, won't they? Do you think people will laugh at us?"

"No. If they are good Christians, they will be glad to see us all walking in."

---

The day simply dragged for Bertha. She felt excited yet very nervous about her pa going to the preaching. She kept thinking about all of the things that might happen at the church, and none of them were good thoughts.

The Bouton boys were excited about going to church since they had never been to a preaching. However, Mary and Bertha were tense on the ride, and James said almost nothing. Walking through the front door was hard for them. *Rosa must have told them we were coming because it doesn't seem like the congregation looks surprised to see us.* People came over and greeted them like they were just regular people.

*Maybe they don't think we are the laughing stock of Liberal after all.*

Several hymns were sung, and Bertha watched her pa, out of the corner of her eye, trying to see if she could tell what he was thinking. Preacher Clark talked about a lot of subjects, and it seemed like everything Pa needed to hear. Bertha saw him wiping tears from his eyes several times.

She kept praying that her pa would go up in front and let them pray with him, but he never got out of his seat. However, everyone seemed happier on the way home, and James told the preacher that they probably would come back.

*Wonder if he just said that to make Ma happy, or will he really be going back?*

When they got home, Bertha took the boys to their bedroom quickly, thinking her parents needed time to have a private visit. She put her head on the pillow and started thinking about everything that had been happening lately. It was almost more than she could even stand to think about. *I've just got to keep praying for peace.*

# Chapter 9

THE NEXT MORNING BROUGHT more surprises to the Bouton home. James sat down with Mary and Bertha in the parlor. With tears in his eyes, he began to talk to them.

"I've a story to tell you. It's one I've never told anyone before," he said slowly. "Pushing it way back in my mind is what I've tried to do for years. I guess I need to get it told and stop letting it ruin my thinking."

Bertha and Mary stared at each other, wondering what they were going to hear next.

"My family was called Christians, and it looked like we were a happy family from the outside. However, there was no happiness in our home. My father was a minister, and all the church folks just thought he was wonderful, but at home he was mean and hateful. I never heard a kind word come from his mouth to my mama or to me or my sisters or brother. But at church, it was like he was a different person. He'd smile and say nice things to everyone and pat little kids on the head. I remember one time my little sister asked our mama why Papa didn't ever smile and pat us kids on the head like he did the kids at church.

"You'd think our mama would have noticed that Papa didn't ever give us kids any affection. She just told my sister to hush up and not be talking bad about Papa 'cause he was a busy, important minister. I wish I could have known my mama when she was younger 'cause maybe she had feelings then. As long as I knew her, she never showed any emotion.

Not happy, not mad, not anything. I'd watch her and wonder if her mind was all right.

It was almost like she didn't have any thoughts of her own, just Papa's thoughts."

James paused, and it seemed hard for him to go on with his story. Bertha and Mary sat still, waiting for him to continue.

"All the time I was growing up, I kept hearing that I was going to be a preacher 'cause my grandfather and father were preachers. I was supposed to follow in their footsteps, but no one asked me what I wanted to be. Every time I heard someone say I was going to be a preacher, something inside of me would say that I didn't want to be a preacher. I wanted to be a doctor. When I got older, I started writing to colleges, asking a lot of questions about what the cost was to go to college. I also asked questions about being a doctor. One day Papa saw a letter that I got back from a college, and he started yelling and screaming at me for even writing to a college. He said I was a terrible son to do things behind his back. Mama just stood there, not saying a word. My little sisters and brother all ran and hid while Papa was yelling at me. For the next two days, Papa was over at the church most of the time, and Mama just went about her work, never speaking or even looking at me. I kept busy trying to help her and hoping she'd want to talk, but she never did. I knew we couldn't go on living in silence and hatred, so I decided to walk over to the church and try to talk to Papa one more time. When I got to the church, no one was in the big meeting room, so I walked back to the room where Papa did his studying. When I opened the door, I got a terrible shock."

James again stopped his story, and it seemed like he just couldn't go on. Mary reached over, patted his hand, and gave him a look that helped him continue.

"There was my papa, the holy preacher, and the lady who played the organ for singing, all wrapped up in each other's arms. I knew for sure they weren't talking about what songs she was planning to be playing at the next preaching. They both jumped apart and looked like they'd seen a ghost. I closed the door, walked home, and was sick to my stomach.

"While wondering what to do next, I blurted out to Mama what I'd just witnessed, and she never even said a word. Just then, Papa came in the house, and his face was red as a beet. I told him that I'd told Mama what I had seen, and if preachers acted that way, I'd never be a preacher. He started yelling at me, accusing me of telling lies about him. I knew what I had seen, and I also knew that papa would never admit he'd done wrong. I just walked into the bedroom, put my things in a little sack, and walked out the door. My brother and sisters were crying, and I really thought Mama or Papa would call me to come back, but they didn't. I had a job at a little store, so I walked over there and asked my boss if I could stay in the back room. I'm sure he wondered why I left home, but he never asked, and I was too ashamed to tell him the real story. I kept working hard, saved every penny I could, and one day I had enough money to go away to school. No one in my family ever stopped by to see me, so when I got on that train, I decided I'd forget about them and become a different person. I changed my name, went to school, and decided to move far away, so I ended up in Missouri. I also decided that someday I'd be the best husband and father that I could possibly be. However, I never wanted to be around Christians 'cause I kept thinking they might be just like my father. When you started going to church and talking about Jesus and love and peace, it got those old bad feelings all stirred up inside of me. However, last night at church, I felt God telling me that just because Papa and Mama didn't show love doesn't mean Jesus doesn't love me. I felt a big ugly burden lift off of me, and I want to tell you how sorry I am for getting involved with that spiritualist business. I know I brought ungodly stuff into our home. It was just a joke, and I really don't know why I wanted to do it. It seemed like a good idea at the time but I know I hurt you both."

By the time James finished his story, Bertha and Mary were also shedding tears. They both jumped up to hug him, and it was a wonderful time, with all the past forgiven.

Looking at Mary, he said, "When I met you and your family, I saw how a true Christian family should be living. I just couldn't seem to forget and forgive my parents.

But last night I did, and I'm going to try to write and find out if my parents are alive.

I'd like to also find my brother and sisters and see if they are all right."

Patting his hand, Mary spoke to him. "That's a good idea, but don't get your hopes up and get hurt all over again."

"I won't get hurt again. I'm a lot older now, and I can take whatever I find out about my family. It'll be good to hear from my brother and sisters. I feel like I just left them to take care of themselves, and I need to see if I can do anything for them."

# Chapter 10

Life in the Bouton home was certainly different now that James had Jesus again. Mary would get out the Bible in the evenings, and she and James would read to the children. As they were reading one evening, they heard a knock on the door, and there stood William Fast. He looked very uncomfortable, and Mary remembered the first time he had ever knocked at that same door, also looking uncomfortable that day.

"Come in, William." They all greeted him at once and invited him to sit with them in the parlor. After a few moments, William blurted out to James, "I'd like your permission to court Bertha. I know she's young and I'm older than her, but I promise to be good to her and do her no harm."

Bertha had known William was going to ask her pa if he could court her. He had whispered his intensions to her at preaching last night. She was surprised that he had come over to the house so soon. *He certainly didn't waste any time.*

She hadn't even had a chance to tell her ma what was on his mind. She thought if Ma was prepared for that question, maybe she could talk to her pa before he came to the house. Everyone sat still, and it seemed like an eternity before James spoke.

"William, I think you are a fine young man, but this is something Mary and I will have to discuss in private. We were just talking about the news of Alice Walser's death. Perhaps you could come back the night of her funeral and stay with Bertha and the boys while Mary accompanies me to the services."

William had not heard the news, so James explained to him that Walser's wife, Alice, had gone to Joplin and taken her own life with poisoning.

"I understand that the funeral will be at midnight, up at their home by Catalpa Park," James stated. "Although we no longer agree on some issues, I do believe that Mary and I should attend this service since he has been a good friend of mine for several years. Maybe I will be able to talk to him at a later date and share some of my thoughts on Christianity. William, perhaps you could drop in that evening and stay with Bertha and her brothers while we will be out late, attending this service. Mary and I will have had time to discuss your request and be prepared to give you an answer."

William replied that he would be happy to stay at their home while they were attending this midnight service. Everyone agreed that midnight was a peculiar time for a funeral.

Bertha was so nervous that she couldn't think of anything to say, and William was just as nervous, so he said good night to the Boutons and left.

The next two days, Bertha was busy cleaning the house and making cookies for William's visit. Wally and Harry were also excited about William coming, and Bertha reminded them several times to be on their best behavior. She wasn't sure what her pa and ma had decided about William courting her, but if Pa asks him to come back and keep her company that night, he surely will say it is all right for him to court her. Ma had mentioned several times that she was just so young, but other girls her age were being courted so maybe they will say yes.

Mary and James left for the funeral; and William, Bertha, and the boys had a wonderful evening, reading and playing games. The boys were enjoying the attention from William and thinking it was great to be able to stay up later than usual. Shortly after midnight, James and Mary returned with a strange report about the funeral. Mr. Walser gave a short speech, and as the casket was lowered into the grave, the clock from the Walser home began striking twelve eerie sounds.

"A chill ran up my spine as that clock struck midnight," Mary declared.

"Then as the dirt was being shoveled into the grave, an owl screeched in the night and took flight over the grave. I've never attended a funeral such as this in all my born days."

James agreed with her. "All of those attending left in complete silence, unable to utter a single word. It's good to be home in warm surroundings after that experience, isn't it, Mary?"

Mary nodded and then looked at James, as if to tell him it was time to give William his answer about courting Bertha.

"We believe that Bertha is certainly young, but you seem to have a good head on your shoulders, William, and we believe that you do have her best interest at heart, so we have decided to give you permission to begin courting our daughter. However, if we feel that you are doing her harm, we will have to amend this decision and ask you to not come to this home anymore."

Giving a big sigh of relief, William grinned at Bertha. "Thank you very much, Mr. and Mrs. Bouton. I'll not make you sorry with this agreement. Tomorrow, being Sunday, could I have Bertha take dinner with my family? And then in the afternoon, we might take a stroll up to Catalpa Park." Looking at Bertha, he added, "That is if Bertha would do me the honor of going to my family dinner and the walk to the park."

Bertha grinned and accepted the date.

"I sure hope that tomorrow will be a sunny day and our walk up to Catalpa Park won't be ruined by any screech owls," Bertha whispered to William as he left to go home.

"Don't worry about tomorrow. You know that on Sunday afternoons the park is always full of young couples enjoying the lake. We will start joining that group every Sunday afternoon, if possible."

---

One day, James and Wally returned from visiting with friends, and they both had smiles on their faces.

"Land's sake," Mary remarked. "You both look like the cat that ate the canary.

What's got you two grinning so much?"

"Sounds like Mr. Walser has Jesus," Wally blurted out.

Mary looked at him, puzzled, and then looked at James for an explanation.

Smiling at Wally and Mary, James said, "The news in Liberal is that Mr. Walser is writing another book, and the title sounds quite interesting. Guess what it is?"

"Well, the way you are smiling, it must not have anything to do with that spiritualist stuff."

"You're right. From what I heard around town, the title is *The Life and Teachings of Jesus*. He described himself as a converted infidel."

"Well, praise be to God" Mary shouted. "He advertised in that little pamphlet that the people in Liberal were the happiest people on earth. Maybe that's true after all."

James looked out the parlor window and saw Bertha and William walking up to their front door. They had been on their usual Sunday afternoon stroll, joining other young couples at Catalpa Park.

"Well, I see two happy people coming in the yard. I'm thinking you had better be thinking about planning a wedding, 'cause I see love written all over their faces."

Mary agreed. "Yes, that is probably the next question William will be asking us, don't you think?"

# Afterword

Bertha Bouton married William Fast on March 29, 1891. The following year their son, Roy, was born. That same year, May 20, 1892, William came in the house from working, complaining of a terrible head ache and suddenly died. Bertha became a seventeen year old widow, with a baby to raise. Her step dad, James Bouton, also died that year. William is buried in the Barton City Cemetery. Bertha and her mother, Mary, both remarried. Bertha married Charles Palmer and they had one son and three daughters. Their youngest daughter was my mother, Gertrude Palmer Hedges. Bertha and Charles lived in Oklahoma for 17 years, returning to Liberal in 1916. The final Liberal house that Bertha lived in was also the first house she and her parents lived in when they moved to Liberal. It is on the southwest corner of Maple and College Street, one block from Main Street. Claude, James, Mary, Wally, Bertha and Charles are buried in the Liberal City Cemetery.

Bertha Bouton, when she was a teen ager.

Bertha and her mother, Mary.

Bertha, when she was a senior citizen.

Bertha in front of the house that she lived in when she first moved to Liberal and it was also the last house she lived in.

MARRIAGE LICENSE.

State of Missouri, County of Barton.

This license authorizes any Judge, Justice of the Peace, licensed or ordained Preacher of the Gospel, or any other person authorized under the Laws of this State, to SOLEMNIZE Marriage between William C. Fast of Barton City Twp County of Barton and State of Mo, who is over the age of twenty-one years, and Miss Bertha Bouton of Ozark Twp County of Barton and State of Mo, who is under the age of eighteen years

The father of said Bertha Bouton gives written consent.

WITNESS my hand as Recorder, with the seal of office hereto affixed, at my office in Lamar, Mo. the 27th day of March 1891.

(L.S.)

J. N. Staats Recorder.

By ____ Deputy.

STATE OF MISSOURI, } ss.
COUNTY OF BARTON. }

THIS IS TO CERTIFY that the undersigned Justice of the Peace did, at Liberal in said County, on the 29th day of March A. D. 1891 unite in Marriage the above named persons.

J. P. Smith J.P.

Filed for Record, this 10th day of April 1891, at 12 o'clock ____ minutes ____ M.

By ____ Deputy. J. N. Staats Recorder.

Bertha and William's marriage license.

William Fast's tombstone, Barton City Cemetery.

James and Mary Bouton's tombstone, Liberal City Cemetery

Bertha Bouton Fast Palmer and Charles Palmer's
tombstone, Liberal City Cemetery

George H. Walser's picture

Liberal City Cemetery, circle in the center of the cemetery, where Walser planned to be buried.

Walser tombstone, Lamar, Missouri, where he was buried.

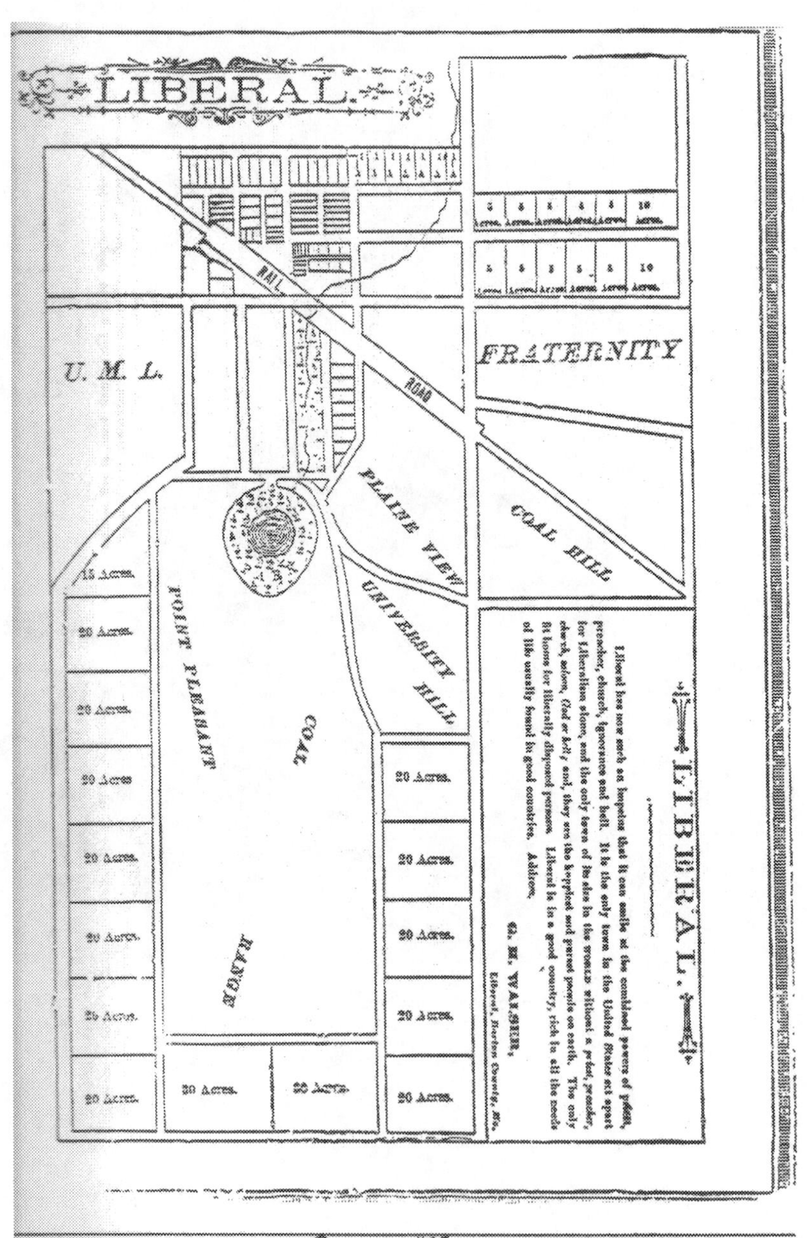


*Document #15*

Liberal plot

Frisco Railroad Depot where Mary and children departed for Pleasant Hill, Mo.

Ozark Hotel which was owned by George Walser

Brown's store where the Bouton family shopped.

Spiritualist camp grounds in Catalpa Park, George Hesford

Spook Hall

Spiritual Science Hall, nicknamed "Spook Hall" and later became the Liberal School agricultural classroom.

Last Residence of G. H. Walser at Catalpa Park

Walser's home in Catalpa Park

# EXPOSES LIBERAL SPIRITUALISTS.

## Liberal's Picturesque Old Man Tells How he and His Friend, the Doctor Worked It—VanCamp Did the Spirit Writing, Himself.

Somebody has gone down to Liberal and written up the town. Not like a real estate agent or a man pulling off a lot sale would have it written up, to be sure, but so that it would be interesting to the readers of Kansas City Sunday Star.

The best part of the story from a point of interest, is the confession made by Uncle Sam VanCamp about the great spiritualist excitement in Liberal something over twenty years ago.

"We cut away the rafters from the roof of a closet in a room in Doctor Bouton's home," he declared. "In the roof we built a trap door and above it between the rafters and the roof a little 'spirit box.' We built everything so carefully that the trap door never was detected though the house was searched by doubters. I was in the spirit box most of the time. We worked the 'slate' gag. The seekers for information gathered in the next room and I had to work quietly. The seeker wrote a question on a slate and Bouton put the slate on a shelf in the closet which opened into the adjoining room. After he closed the door I reached down, took the slate and wrote the answer. We found out as much about everybody as possible so that our answers would ring true. I don't remember what they asked, but many of them had to be thought about before answering. I had to work quickly and on top of it was the fear of detection. But that's what made it glorious sport. After replacing the slate I rapped and Bouton opened the door. From the murmurs as he read the answer I could tell how well I had guessed.

"One time," continued Van Camp after relighting his pipe, "we were nearly caught. So many customers came that we had to work faster. I kept several slates with answers already written with me and when Bouton put a slate on the shelf, I replaced it with an appropriate answer. The time I have in mind, I just had put one of the answer slates on the shelf and rapped for Bouton, when I noticed with horror that the slate I had put down was much larger than the other. I reached down quickly to correct the mistake, when Bouton opened the door. Instantly he shut it, but the audience had seen my hand descending. I thought it was all up, but Bouton, with rare presence of mind, calmly explained that the spirit hand had not finished writing. 'What a pretty hand that was,' I heard a woman say. 'Just like an angel's.' That made us stronger than ever. More people came, and we had to put a larger plate at the door."

Reprint from the Lamar Democrat, 1910